MURDER AT THE PALACE PIER

A LADY ELIZABETH HAWTHORNE MYSTERY
OLIVIA ROSE

Copyright © 2025 by Olivia Rose

All rights reserved.

No part of this publication may be reproduced, distributed, or transmitted in any form or by any means, including photo-copying, recording, or other electronic or mechanical methods, without the prior written permission of the publisher, except as permitted by U.S. copyright law. For permission requests, contact [include publisher/author contact info].

The story, all names, characters, and incidents portrayed in this production are fictitious. No identification with actual persons (living or deceased), places, buildings, and products is intended or should be inferred.

Publisher: Olivia Rose

Lady Elizabeth Hawthorne - Family Tree

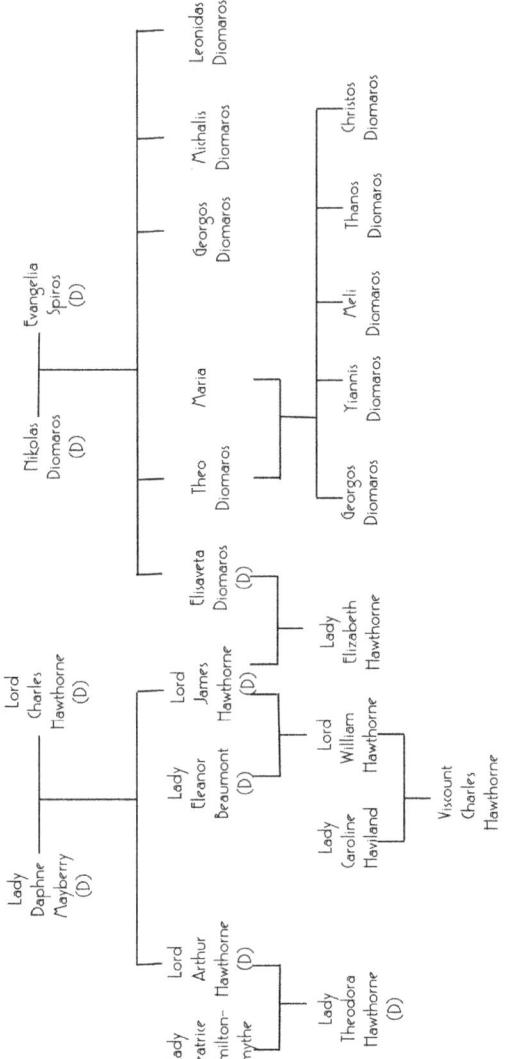

Contents

Chapter One	1
Chapter Two	14
Chapter Three	31
Chapter Four	45
Chapter Five	54
Chapter Six	67
Chapter Seven	76
Chapter Eight	84
Chapter Nine	93
Chapter Ten	105
Chapter Eleven	115
Chapter Twelve	129
Chapter Thirteen	137
Chapter Fourteen	149

Chapter Fifteen	165
Chapter Sixteen	175
Chapter Seventeen	187
Chapter Eighteen	201
Chapter Nineteen	211
Chapter Twenty	218
Chapter Twenty-One	226
Chapter Twenty-Two	233
Chapter Twenty-Three	246
Epilogue	253
Dedication	259
Also by Olivia Rose	260
About the Author	280

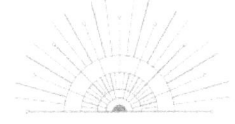

Chapter One

THE BRIGHTON EXPRESS EASED from Victoria Station in a hiss of steam, white smoke billowing past the windows as it threaded through the maze of signal boxes and points. Elizabeth watched the station's soaring iron and glass roof fade into the distance, replaced by the tightly packed terraces and chimney stacks of South London.

June sunlight streamed through the windows, warming the air despite the morning's early hour. Meli sat opposite, her gaze fixed on the passing landscape. Beyond the glass, rows of terraced houses and factory chimneys slowly surrendered to red-brick homes with their neat gardens. The usual sparkle had vanished from her toffee-coloured eyes, replaced by an uncharacteristic weariness that spoke of her father's ultimatum – return to Athens or remain in London without their financial support.

Elizabeth recognised her uncle's words for what they were – an empty threat. She knew he wouldn't truly withdraw Meli's allowance, but Aunt Maria's yearning for their only daughter's return had forced his hand. In Meli's desire for independence, Elizabeth saw her own determination to forge a path beyond society's narrow expectations, but she'd kept her counsel. The decision must be Meli's alone.

"A penny for your thoughts?"

Meli turned from the window, lips parting before she caught herself. "Tell me about your cousin Gigi. Is she really as wild as Aunt Beatrice claims?"

Elizabeth laughed. "Hardly. Though I suppose her upbringing wasn't quite what Aunt Beatrice had in mind for her niece, the Honourable Genevieve Hamilton-Smythe."

"Ah yes, your uncle Auggy. The infamous black sheep."

"Poor Uncle Auggy, he's such a dear and the furthest thing from a black sheep one could find."

"Then why does Aunt Beatrice look so pained whenever his name is mentioned?"

Elizabeth settled back against the velvet moquette as the Surrey countryside gave way to Sussex as the train pressed south. Villages appeared and vanished, each a glimpse of English life with its church spire and cluster of homes set among rolling hills. Gardens and village greens flashed past the window while sheep grazed the distant slopes, the landscape shifting with each passing mile.

"Because his marriage to Aunt Celeste caused quite the scandal. She wasn't at all the sort of match Victorian society expected for a Hamilton-Smythe. Though Aunt Beatrice adores her now, she hasn't forgotten those barbed comments from society's elite."

"Was she Italian? Is that why they moved to Tuscany?"

"No, she was his nurse at the London hospital where he was being treated after a nasty bout of asthma. Neither the London air nor society agreed with Uncle Auggy, and the lure of Tuscany's milder climate and landscapes proved too tempting. Aunt Beatrice was quite put out and spent years trying to persuade them to let Gigi return to England and live with her at Hawthorne Hall."

Meli's eyes widened. "Aunt Beatrice wanted to adopt Gigi?"

"Of course not, she simply wanted to give Gigi a proper English finishing, befitting a well-bred young lady."

"Did she? Return to Hawthorne Hall, I mean?"

"No, when war broke out, they decided she would be safer in Tuscany than in England. And with Uncle Auggy and Aunt Celeste having converted several of the villa's outbuildings into convalescent wards, it was a case of all-hands-on-deck – no matter how small."

"Will Gigi's parents be at the Brighton house?"

"It's unlikely; summer's always busy at the villa. Uncle Auggy took up painting after they moved to Tuscany, and now the old outbuildings serve as something of an artist's retreat."

"Gigi made the journey from Tuscany by herself?" Meli's brows arched, her voice tinged with awe.

"For someone who travelled halfway across the Mediterranean Sea as a stowaway, you sound rather impressed by Gigi's solo travel arrangements."

"That was different." Meli's shoulders dropped as she sank back into the upholstery. "I knew Mama and Papa would never have given their permission for me to accompany you to London, so what choice did I have?"

Elizabeth's head rolled back as she studied her cousin from beneath her lashes. While she understood Meli's frustration, she knew Aunt Maria's protective instincts came from love rather than any desire to clip her daughter's wings. Still, hiding aboard a steamship had been an extreme solution, even by Meli's standards.

"Did I ever tell you about Gigi's first week in Tuscany?" Elizabeth leaned forward, a smile tugging at the corner of her mouth. "She convinced the entire village she was Princess Mary's secret younger sister, sent to stay with the Hamilton-Smythes for safekeeping. Poor Uncle Auggy couldn't understand why everyone kept curtseying until someone showed him the Italian newspaper announcing that the Hamilton-Smythes were secretly hosting a British royal for the summer."

"She did not!" Meli bolted upright, her eyes brightening. "Was her father very angry?"

"Far from it. He found it rather amusing, though he insisted she write a letter of apology to the newspaper." Elizabeth launched into another tale of Gigi's escapades as they passed through Clayton Tunnel, this one involving a runaway donkey and the local priest's prized vegetable garden.

Preston Park's neat gardens and tree-lined avenues marked their entry into Brighton proper. Elizabeth's tales of Gigi's Tuscan adventures carried them through the final miles, her cousin's laughter filling their compartment.

The station's iron and glass canopy stretched above them like a vast Victorian conservatory as they neared Brighton Station. Steam hissed and wheels clattered against iron tracks as the train eased to a halt alongside the platform.

A porter in his crisp navy uniform and peaked cap stepped forward as Elizabeth unlatched the carriage door. "Porter, miss?"

"Thank you, that would be splendid." Elizabeth's gaze swept their compartment one last time before stepping down to join Meli on the platform. "We have two cases in the guards' van, brown leather with the initials E.H. in gold."

"Very good, miss. If you'd follow me, please."

Elizabeth and Meli wove between the clusters of lively holidaymakers and excited children, dodging brass-wheeled trolleys piled high with steamer trunks and valises as they tried to keep pace with their porter. Two small boys in matching caps dashed between them, ducking the pink geraniums and trailing purple petunias cascading from metal baskets hanging between the pillars, while the station clock above the booking office marked half-past eleven.

Elizabeth yanked Meli aside as a porter's trolley laden with trunks cut across their path. "The station's rather busy this morning."

"Summer season always brings the crowds, miss. But I swear it gets busier every year. Perhaps it's better if you wait at the cab stand while I fetch your cases?"

Elizabeth threaded her way between waiting passengers toward the cab stand, Meli close behind. "Can you see your cousin?"

"Gigi embraces the Italian way." Elizabeth's lips curved into a smile. "*Piano, piano*."

"*Piano, piano*?"

"Just like our *siga, siga*."

"Ah." Meli chuckled. "Slowly, slowly."

MWEEP! MWEEP! MWEEP! MWEEP!

Heads turned as a carmine red Vauxhall 23-60 Tourer raced across the forecourt, a violet splash visible above the windscreen. One hand gripped the steering wheel, the other outstretched, sweeping the air in greeting.

The Vauxhall lurched sideways to avoid an oncoming Austin. Gigi twisted in her seat, both hands leaving the wheel. "Sorry! I'm so sorry!"

"As you can see." Elizabeth arched a brow. "My cousin has a little trouble remembering which side of the road she should be driving on."

The Vauxhall jolted to a stop before them. Gigi flung open the door, her copper hair bright beneath a violet silk scarf knotted at her ear. "Elizabeth!" She caught Elizabeth in a whirl of Italian perfume and continental kisses. "It's been an age since I last saw you."

"It has indeed." Elizabeth stepped back, taking in the sun-kissed glow of her cousin's face, the sparkle of mischief in her grey-green eyes. "And how are Uncle Auggy and Aunt Celeste?"

"Up to their elbows in cherries, no doubt. The *Sagra delle Ciliegie* takes over the entire village. And you must be Meli." Another swift embrace followed, accompanied by a kiss on each cheek. "I've read so much about you in Elizabeth's letters I feel I know you already."

"And I, you, after Elizabeth's stories."

"Elizabeth, you didn't tell her the Princess Mary story, did you?" Gigi tipped back her head with a laugh. "Papa still has that newspaper clipping framed in his study." She turned to the beautiful, dark-haired woman alighting from the passenger seat with far more grace than Gigi had. "And this is my dearest friend, Essie."

Essie extended her hand to Elizabeth, then Meli, dimples forming in her cheeks as her smile widened. "Old Signora Bianchi at the *pas-*

ticceria always slips me an extra slice of *panforte di Siena* whenever I go there, for the *principessa*."

"Take no notice of Essie, she's just jealous because Signora Bianchi never saves her a free slice." Gigi's hand fluttered in dismissal.

The station clock struck quarter to twelve as Elizabeth's gaze swept the platform. Catching sight of the porter steering his trolley through the morning crowd, she beckoned him over with a small wave.

"Back again so soon, Miss?" The porter swung both cases onto the metal rack at the rear of the motorcar, tightening the leather straps until the buckles lay flat.

"Mr Jenkins." Gigi's eyes crinkled at the corners. "Excellent timing, as usual."

He gave each case a firm shake, checking it was secure. "There you go, Miss." He stepped back, touching his cap.

Elizabeth pressed a half-crown into his palm. "Thank you for your help, Mr Jenkins."

"Most generous, my lady. Thank you." He touched his cap once more.

"All aboard!" Gigi slid behind the wheel, adjusting her driving gloves as the Vauxhall's engine purred to life beneath her touch.

"You make sure you mind that coast road, miss, especially with all the extra traffic about."

"Don't fret, Mr Jenkins, we'll be as safe as the Bank of England!" Gigi's voice carried back as she pulled away from the kerb.

Essie's hand flew to her hat as they rounded the first corner. She twisted in her seat to face Elizabeth and Meli in the back. "You might want to hold on to your hats, ladies ... quite literally."

A delivery van's horn blared as they exited the cab stand. Gigi raised one hand in cheerful acknowledgement as she swerved across to the correct side without missing a beat in her conversation.

"I thought we might take the scenic route past the seafront." The car swooped down the slope of Queens Road, where seagulls wheeled between the elegant facades. At the bottom of the hill, the English Channel sparkled like cut glass in the June sunshine.

Turning left onto Kings Road, they joined the steady stream of seafront traffic. Holidaymakers dotted the promenade, where cordyline palms stood in neat ranks beside formal flowerbeds bright with geraniums and marigolds. Gigi accelerated past a horse-drawn cab, cutting back in with inches to spare. Elizabeth's stomach lurched as the horse tossed its head, the driver's indignant shout lost in the purr of the Vauxhall's engine.

The grand curve of Adelaide Crescent opened before them, a sweep of cream-painted houses. The end-of-terrace townhouse stood proud in pale stucco, its tall sash windows with slender glazing bars stretching up three storeys. The black-painted front door sat beneath a shallow portico with slender columns, its fanlight etched with a swirling pattern. A decorative ironwork balcony graced the first-floor window, while tessellated tiles lined the short path between the low railings.

At the side of the end-of-terrace house, Gigi steered the Vauxhall through the iron gates, wheels crunching over the gravel as she guided the motorcar along the narrow drive. Pink rose bushes spilled over the garden wall on one side, while the converted coach house stood before them, its double doors already open.

Gigi eased the Vauxhall inside. "Don't worry about the cases, Mr B will see to them. I must dash. I need to speak to Mrs B about eating earlier tonight." She slipped from behind the wheel and took two steps before turning back. "Oh, did I mention we're going dancing tonight? At The Lux." Without waiting for an answer, she hurried along the stone path towards the house.

Essie's shoulders dropped as she released a long breath. "At least there's less chance of her killing us on the dance floor."

"Indeed." Elizabeth unclenched her fingers from the seat in front and glanced across at Meli, her Mediterranean complexion tinged green. "It's all right, you can open your eyes now."

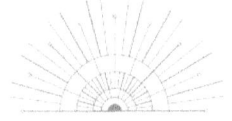

Chapter Two

Voile panels stirred in the salt-tinged breeze as weary voices drifted up from the promenade. Below, sun-drowsy families made their way to lodging houses and hotels, while the last ice cream vendor called to the remaining beach-goers as Brighton Pier's lights flickered to life against the violet sky.

Meli sat at the dressing table, catching Elizabeth's eye in the triptych mirror as she applied her coral lipstick. "Have you been to The Lux before?"

"I haven't, not since its conversion." Elizabeth leaned forward on the edge of the bed as she fastened the strap of her silver beaded evening shoe. "I believe it was a butcher's shop the last time I was here."

"A butcher's shop?" Meli paused mid-swipe, her lipstick hovering above her lips. "But Gigi says it's the most fashionable spot in Brighton. She said that everyone who's anyone goes dancing at The Lux."

Elizabeth held Meli's gaze in the mirror, a smile tugging at the corners of her mouth. "I hardly think they've kept the sawdust floor and meat hooks. Although…" She tapped her chin with a fingertip. "I suppose they might come in handy for hanging one's coat."

"Elizabeth!" Meli chuckled, sliding a jewelled peacock clip into her dark curls. "Now I shan't be able to stop thinking about sides of beef all evening."

The bright refrains of "Everybody Loves My Baby" drifted up the stairs, the piano riff echoing through the house. Elizabeth twisted in the full-length mirror, midnight blue silk swirling around her calves, silver beading catching the light like stars scattered across a twilight sky. "It sounds like Gigi is getting in a little practice before we leave."

"I can't say I blame her." Meli's fingers tapped against the dressing table as she rose, the melody drawing her into a shimmy across the room. In the full-length mirror, she smoothed the tiers of gold-threaded fringe at her hip, swaying in time to the rhythm. Fine beadwork traced the neckline, while a daring low back and slender straps left her shoulders almost bare – a bold splash of coral against her Mediterranean colouring. "It feels like an age since I last went dancing."

"We should head down." Elizabeth gathered her silver-beaded evening bag from the bed. "Before Gigi sends a search party."

The lively beats of "Ain't We Got Fun" filled the house as they entered the sitting-room. Gigi spun between the sage-coloured armchairs, her jade green Jeanne Lanvin gown a blur in the gilt-edged mirror above the fireplace.

"At last." She caught Meli's hands, pulling her into a shimmy and step, their fringed dresses swishing in time. Coral and jade threads shimmered as they moved across the oak floor. "We thought perhaps you'd changed your minds, and were about to leave without you, weren't we, Essie?"

"Don't be such a tease." Essie smiled from her corner of the sofa, the dove-grey silk of her dress falling in soft pleats to her ankles.

"Now that our slowcoaches have finally joined us..." Gigi twirled across the room to the gramophone, lifting the needle from the spinning disc. "Shall we make a move, ladies?"

"Are you sure you'll be warm enough with this?" Mrs Bramley bustled into the sitting-room, Gigi's freshly pressed chiffon wrap draped over her arm. "That sea breeze has a nasty nip to it once the sun goes down."

"Oh, Mrs B, it's a hundred degrees out there." Gigi accepted the wrap with a quick kiss to Mrs Bramley's cheek. "We'll be perfectly fine, I assure you."

"Are you sure you won't need your coats, Lady Elizabeth?" Mrs Bramley eyed Meli's bare shoulders. "I can have Lily run up and fetch them, it won't take but a minute."

Elizabeth touched Mrs Bramley's arm, the gesture as warm as her smile. "Thank you, but we're perfectly fine, Mrs Bramley."

Mrs Bramley settled the chiffon wrap around Gigi's shoulders.

"Thank you." Gigi squeezed Mrs Bramley's hand before gesturing towards the hall. "Shall we?"

They crossed the hall to the front door, Elizabeth, Meli and Essie making their way to the taxi idling beyond the wrought-iron gate. Gigi paused on the top step, turning back to Mrs Bramley. "Now, I don't want you waiting up, fretting all evening."

"Of course I'll be waiting up. What would I say to your parents if anything happened while I was tucked up in the land of nod?"

"Oh, Mrs B." Gigi shook her head, smiling as she descended the steps. "You do worry so."

Gigi slipped into the seat beside Elizabeth, arranging her beaded skirt as she settled back against the leather upholstery.

"Poor Mrs B, she's such a worrier." They returned Mrs Bramley's wave as the taxi pulled away from Adelaide Crescent. "I missed her and Mr B dreadfully when we first moved to Tuscany. Mama and Papa tried everything to persuade them to come with us, but Mrs B refused. She said as much as she'd miss us, Brighton was home, and that was that."

"Where to, ladies?" The driver glanced in his mirror.

"The Lux, please," Gigi replied.

"Very good, miss."

The taxi wound through Brighton's evening streets, past children trailing sand buckets while their parents carried sleeping toddlers homeward. The Grand Hotel spilled light and jazz onto the promenade, where evening dress had replaced bathing suits, and cigarettes glowed like fireflies. The sea breeze swept through the driver's half-open window, carrying the sound of waves lapping against the shingle shoreline as they followed Marine Parade, where a lone lamplighter worked his way along the row of street lamps.

The taxi drew to a halt just before The Lux, where a quartet of young men in lounge suits descended the steps beside them, a burst of trumpet floating up the stairwell through the open door.

"How much?" Gigi opened her evening bag.

"That'll be two and six, miss."

"Thank you." She placed the coins in his palm.

He opened his fingers, eyes widening at the five shillings. "Thank you, miss." He touched his cap. "Very kind of you, miss."

The cab rattled over the cobbles as it joined the steady stream of motorcars and carriages making their way towards Kings Road.

Gigi led the way down the stone steps, pushing open the green front door to the lively beat of "Yes! We Have No Bananas" pulsing from the jazz ensemble inside.

Elizabeth took in the velvet booths along the back wall, the dance floor packed with bright young things cutting loose, the bar with its silver cocktail shakers and mirrored backdrop displaying bottles of every description.

Gigi hesitated, her gaze sweeping the tables. "Over there." She lifted her hand in greeting to a fair-haired young man seated in one of the private booths along the rear wall.

They followed as Gigi led the way with the ease of a seasoned regular, stopping to greet fellow revellers as she went.

"Rather glamorous for an old cold storage, wouldn't you say?" Elizabeth dipped her head closer to Meli's ear. "And not a single meat hook or side of beef in sight."

"Indeed." Meli chuckled. "Although I must confess, I was half expecting sawdust floors, despite Gigi's claims about it being the most fashionable spot in Brighton."

The jazz band shifted tempo as they approached the booth, the clarinet weaving between the piano notes. The fair-haired young man set down his champagne glass, rising to greet them.

"Late as usual," a dark-haired woman with a sleek Eton crop, and attired in ivory silk that whispered of Parisian ateliers, drawled from behind a veil of cigarette smoke.

"Fashionably so, of course." Gigi met the barb with a dazzling smile before stretching up to press a kiss to the man's cheek. "Happy birthday, Tommy."

"Thank you, darling." Tommy reached for the champagne bottle nestled in the silver ice bucket, filling four glasses and signalling to a waiter for more. "Aren't you going to introduce us to your charming friends?"

"Honestly, Tommy." Gigi rolled her eyes before sweeping an arm around the group. "This is Eustace Grimwald." She indicated the raven-haired young man with an easy smile.

"Stacey, please." He raised his left hand in greeting. "Only my father calls me Eustace."

"Ah yes, Mr Justice Grimwald." The dark-haired woman blew smoke from the corner of her mouth. "What is it they say? Grim by name, grim by nature?"

Gigi's fingers tightened on her clutch. "And this is Rosalind Delacourt."

Rosalind lifted her glass, inclined her head, and drained the contents as everyone settled into their seats.

"Sylvia Carlton and her husband Markus." Gigi's gesture took in the couple – Markus in a burgundy velvet jacket and cravat despite the June heat, Sylvia in a dress that spoke of an expert eye making the most of last season's lines.

"These are my cousins, Lady Elizabeth Hawthorne and Miss Meli Diomaros."

"Pleased to meet you." Sylvia tilted her head, her dark eyes crinkling at the corners. "Is this your first time in Brighton?"

"No, I'm quite familiar with Brighton, but it's Meli's first visit."

"So you're a frequent visitor?" Markus held Elizabeth's gaze. "But I suppose Brighton does have the reputation for being the preserve of those who have nothing to do, and all day to do it in."

"Elizabeth idle?" Gigi turned to Markus. "Hardly. She's made quite a name for herself as a detective."

"Detective?" Markus's lips twitched. "What sort of detecting? Missing hat pins and misplaced gloves?"

"Murder, actually." Gigi arched an eyebrow over her champagne glass.

"Really?" Rosalind's cigarette paused halfway to her lips.

"Gigi's exaggerating; it wasn't all me. Meli also played her part."

"Finally, someone interesting to talk to. Slide over, would you, Stacey?" Rosalind made room on the banquette, patting the space beside her. "Now, you must tell me everything."

Meli slipped into the space beside Rosalind while Gigi continued, "And you all know Essie, of course."

"We do indeed." Tommy brushed a kiss across Essie's knuckles. "Looking as gorgeous as ever."

Rosalind's shoulders tensed as she ground her cigarette into the crystal ashtray.

Essie withdrew her hand with a smile. "Really, Tommy, you're incorrigible."

"You'd better watch yourself, Tommy." Rosalind reached for another cigarette, tapping it against her holder. "You wouldn't want Essie's beau to get the wrong idea, would you?"

Essie's gaze slid to the dance floor. "I don't have a beau."

"That's not what the society pages say." Rosalind drew on her cigarette, smoke curling between them.

"The society pages are mistaken."

"According to Mrs Drummond-Ward's column – and she's hardly ever wrong – you and Mr Laurence Pembroke are quite the item. And you know what they say, where there's smoke..."

"Perhaps *they* should concern themselves less with gossip and attend to their own affairs." Essie's fingers curled against her clutch as she pushed back from the table and stood. "If you'll excuse me. I'm in need of some fresh air."

"Really, Rosalind?" Gigi sprang to her feet, watching Essie make her way towards the entrance. "Did you have to?"

"It's not my fault she's so sensitive." Rosalind tapped her cigarette holder against the ashtray. "I was only repeating what everyone else has been saying for weeks. It's hardly a secret, is it?"

"Essie's a private person, Rosalind. She doesn't court attention like–"

"Like me?"

Gigi's shoulders sagged as she let out a sigh. "I didn't say that."

"You didn't have to." Rosalind tilted her head back, exhaling a perfect smoke ring into the air. "Anyway, I don't know why you're making such a fuss, it was only a bit of fun. How was I to know she'd get herself all in a tizzy over it?"

"Clearly, Essie didn't see it that way." Gigi glanced towards the entrance. "I should check on her."

Elizabeth caught Meli's eye, the faint furrow in her cousin's brow mirroring her own discomfort.

"Swingin' Down the Lane" spilled from the jazz band. Stacey swayed in time with the music. "Would you care to dance?" he asked, turning to Meli. "Though I can't promise not to step on your toes."

"Then I'll just have to take my chances."

"Rosalind, would you mind…?" Stacey gestured to the end of the banquette. "It's easier for you to move than for Sylvia and Markus."

Rosalind muttered something under her breath, snatching up her silver cigarette case and beaded evening bag. She slid off the banquette with a sharp tug at her skirt.

"Where are you going?" Tommy asked.

"Where do you think?" She brushed past his shoulder, her chin high as she headed towards the bar.

"And then there were four."

Sylvia flicked a glance at her husband, one brow lifting in quiet reproof, before turning to Elizabeth. "Pay no attention to Rosalind, she can be a little ... prickly, but I'm sure she didn't mean anything by it."

"Ignore Sylvia." Tommy grinned in Sylvia's direction. "She has the infuriating habit of always seeing the good in everyone." His mouth twisted as his gaze snapped to Markus. "Even in those who don't deserve it."

"More champagne, anyone?" Sylvia reached for the bottle.

Elizabeth shook her head, her gaze sweeping the crowds for any sign of Gigi or Essie.

She spotted Gigi hovering beside a table of acquaintances, her smile bright as she exchanged greetings, though her attention kept straying to the entrance.

Behind Gigi, on the other side of the club, Elizabeth caught sight of Essie. A man with slicked-back hair and a rumpled suit stood in front of her, a Box Brownie camera clutched in his hands. Essie's shoulders drew back, her chin lifting as she took a half-step away. One hand rose between them, palm out.

Elizabeth turned to Sylvia, nodding toward the man with the camera. "Do you know who that man is? Over there with Essie."

Sylvia shifted in her seat, peering between dancing couples and clusters of standing patrons, just as the photographer stepped sideways, deliberately blocking Essie's path. He raised his camera again, the black box aimed at her face. Essie twisted her head away, one hand raised in protest. When she tried once more to step around him, he mirrored her movement, cutting off her escape.

Sylvia leaned closer to Elizabeth's ear, her voice rising above the music. "That's Jimmy Morton. He works for those scandal sheets. He's always hanging around places like this, lurking in the shadows hoping to catch people in compromising situations or with someone they shouldn't be. And when he can't find a genuine story, he simply creates one."

Elizabeth reached for her bag, ready to go after Essie when she spotted Gigi beside her, arm linked through Essie's as she guided her towards one of the quieter alcoves.

She settled back into her seat as a broad-shouldered man in a well-cut black suit appeared at the photographer's side. His expression remained pleasant, almost cordial, as he bent to speak in Morton's ear. The photographer's face flushed, his mouth opening to protest, but the suited man's grip tightened visibly on his shoulder as he guided him through the crowd. They moved in tandem towards the entrance, the taller man's smile never faltering as he steered Morton out the door.

Elizabeth watched the door swing shut behind Morton, her gaze drifting to the alcove where Gigi comforted Essie.

She tried to recall Gigi's letters and whether they'd contained any mention of Essie, but her mind drew a blank.

The close bond shared between Gigi and Essie was undeniable, and yet Gigi had never mentioned Essie before. Nor that she'd be joining them in Brighton.

Why had Essie bristled so at Rosalind's mention of society column speculation about Laurence Pembroke being her beau?

Was Essie's Mr Pembroke the same progressive Liberal tipped to unseat the Tory incumbent in the upcoming election?

Could he be the reason Morton had been pestering Essie?

Gigi had claimed Essie was a private person who shunned attention, yet Laurence Pembroke was a rising star in British politics.

Was Gigi right about Essie being shy?

Or was it public scrutiny rather than attention the beautiful Miss Baker shied away from?

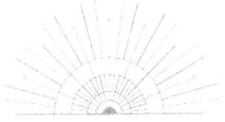

Chapter Three

GULLS SWOOPED OVERHEAD, THEIR cries carrying over the steady clip of the milk cart's wheels on the Brighton cobbles. Outside the open window, deep pink geraniums and soft mauve sweet peas climbed the coach house wall, while Mr Bramley weaved through his wife's herb beds, selecting sprigs of rosemary and thyme for the evening meal.

Elizabeth shifted in her chair, last night's questions about Essie circling in her mind. Across the breakfast table, Gigi had folded herself onto the chair like a cat, bare feet tucked beneath the folds of her embroidered silk kimono. She tore another piece from her *ciambella*, the sugar dusting her fingers as she devoured it.

"Gigi…" Elizabeth set down her teacup. "About Essie–"

"Did someone mention my name?" Essie appeared in the doorway.

"Ah, talk of the devil." Gigi unfolded herself from her chair. "Are you feeling better this morning?"

Essie crossed to the gilt-framed mirror above the fireplace, adjusting the angle of her cloche. "Just a touch of grogginess, but the fresh air should help clear it."

"Meli and I are heading out for a walk shortly, why don't you join us?"

"Oh, I wouldn't want to impose." She avoided Elizabeth's gaze in the mirror.

"Not at all, we'd love to have you join us."

"That's very kind of you, but I have a couple of errands to run."

"We'd be happy to tag along, we're in no great rush."

"No, really. They're such tedious errands, and I couldn't bear to waste your morning, especially on such a glorious day." Essie turned from the mirror, her smile a shade too bright, as she exited the morning-room. "I'd better get on."

Elizabeth waited for Essie's footsteps to fade. "At least she seems more herself this morning."

"Essie's resilient." Gigi tore off another piece of *ciambella*. "But because she's so reserved, people assume she's fragile."

"Rosalind certainly seemed determined to unsettle her last night."

"She can't resist stirring things up." Gigi waved her hand, scattering more sugar. "Best not to give her the satisfaction of a reaction."

Elizabeth recalled the previous evening and how Rosalind had taken pleasure in seeing Essie's distress, like a cat toying with a mouse.

"She's not so terrible, really, not when you get to know her." Gigi settled deeper into her chair. "Just too much money and time on her hands, I suppose."

"You've known her long?"

"Since we were girls. Before Papa whisked us off to Tuscany." Gigi brushed sugar from her lips. "More tea?"

Elizabeth shook her head. "And Essie? Did you meet her here in Brighton?"

"No, actually. In Tuscany." Gigi reached for her cup.

"Rather far from home for a young English woman."

"She'd been working for the Contessa Visconti as a governess to her girls, but there was some disagreement about wages, I think it was, and she was dismissed. With no family in England, she stayed in Tuscany, modelling for local artists. When Jasper Vale first laid eyes on her, he declared he wouldn't paint anyone else, and since he was staying with us at the villa, it made sense for Essie to stay there too. We hit it off immediately and have been friends ever since."

"Jasper Vale the artis–"

"Oh! That reminds me." Gigi rose from her chair. "Vale's exhibiting at the Palace Pier Exhibition Rooms tonight. I promised Stacey we'd make an appearance." She stretched lazily. "I do so miss the swimming pool on a day like this. But since I'm in Brighton and not Tuscany, I suppose a cold bath will have to suffice."

Elizabeth watched her cousin leave, turning Gigi's words over in her mind. Norland nannies were highly sought after, their references scrutinised with care. For the Contessa to let Essie go over a wages dispute...

"Ready?" Meli paused in the doorway, adjusting the lace on her summer gloves.

Elizabeth pushed back from the breakfast table. "Just let me fetch my hat."

She adjusted the angle of her wide-brimmed hat against the sun as they stepped outside, her mind still circling the previous evening's events involving Essie. Gigi, so kind and openhearted, had a history of collecting stray kittens and injured birds ever since childhood – and something about her cousin's friendship with Essie troubled Elizabeth, but she couldn't put her finger on the reason why.

Purple stems brushed against their legs as they followed the gravel path through the communal gardens, filling the air with the scent of lavender. Between tumbling beds of peonies and foxgloves, a ginger cat had claimed the stone edging as its throne, watching through half-closed eyes as two sparrows squabbled over territory among the rose bushes.

"You're quiet this morning." Meli linked her arm through Elizabeth's.

"Just a little tired after such an early start and late night yesterday." She wasn't ready to voice her concerns about Essie, not when they were based on nothing more than a feeling. "You seemed to enjoy yourself last night. I hardly saw you – you spent most of the evening dancing with Stacey."

Meli caught her heel on a raised paving slab and stumbled, steadying herself against Elizabeth's arm with a wince. "My toes are a little tender this morning."

"Well, he did give you fair warning."

"He did indeed, but he's so nice, I didn't have the heart to complain, and tried to time every groan with the change in tempo."

A smile twitched at the corners of Elizabeth's mouth as they crossed to Western Road, sidestepping a delivery boy zigzagging through the foot traffic with a parcel slung under one arm.

Meli held out her hand, flexing her fingers as she turned it. "Did you notice Stacey's right hand?"

"I can't say I did."

"The fourth and fifth fingers curve inward. Rather unusual, isn't it?"

"Perhaps it's the result of an accident?"

"Perhaps."

Beyond Regency Square, Brighton Palace Pier stretched out over the water, its central dome and iron fretwork silhouetted against the summer sky. The tide was in, waves slapping against the pilings beneath the holiday crowds.

"What did you make of Rosalind's behaviour last night?" Meli's gaze followed a gull's swooping descent.

"How do you mean?"

"The way she treated Essie, and those constant digs at poor Sylvia – everything from her dress to her position at Hannington's."

"Yes, she seemed to have an opinion on everything."

"Thank goodness Tommy kept her on the dance floor most of the night and away from Rosalind."

Elizabeth shook her head. "Perhaps that wasn't the saving grace you think it was."

"What do you mean?"

"Didn't you notice how Rosalind's barbs were aimed solely at the women Tommy paid attention to?"

Meli paused mid-step. "I'd thought her behaviour was because of all the champagne she'd drunk, but now that you mention it…"

"I suspect there's more than simple spite behind Rosalind's sharp tongue."

They passed through the wrought-iron gates and decorative archway of Brighton's Palace Pier. The wooden decking stretched over the English Channel, its boards worn smooth by countless visitors.

The June sunshine had drawn crowds from far and wide to the East Sussex coast. Ladies in summer frocks twirled parasols against the heat, while children darted between deck chairs clutching paper bags of peppermint rock.

Elizabeth's gaze travelled the length of the pier, following the gentle curve of railings out over the water. "Shall we explore the pier now, or stop for tea first?"

"I could murder a cup of tea." Meli shifted her weight from one foot to the other, her lips tightening at the corners. "And my feet could do with a rest."

The Palace Pier Tea Rooms commanded the corner of the pier, its white-painted façade and tall windows a welcome oasis. Elizabeth turned towards the entrance, but Meli caught her arm.

"Look – isn't that Stacey Grimwald?"

A few yards ahead, a young man in a rumpled linen suit wrestled with several large canvases, each wrapped in brown paper. As Elizabeth watched, one slipped sideways, threatening to escape his grip.

"Mr Grimwald?" Elizabeth quickened her pace. "Do you need a hand?"

"Lady Elizabeth!" His dark hair fell across his forehead as he adjusted his precarious hold. "I wouldn't dream of – oh, blast." The smallest canvas made a bid for freedom.

Elizabeth caught it before it hit the boards. "There. No harm done."

"Thank you." He adjusted his grip on the canvases, steadying the paintings against his side. "And Miss Diomaros – how are those toes this morning?"

"In fine fettle."

"Delighted to hear it, I was worried I'd disfigured you for life."

"Not at all." Meli nodded towards the wrapped canvases, avoiding Elizabeth's gaze. "Are these for tonight's exhibition?"

"Indeed, they are." A flush crept up his neck. "Though displaying alongside Jasper Vale feels rather like a sparrow perching next to a peacock."

"Nonsense." Meli replied. "The gallery proprietor must think otherwise, or they wouldn't have included you."

"Ah." Stacey's smile turned wry. "I'm afraid that's more to do with her friendship with my mother than any merit of mine. They were quite close before..."

"Oh, I'm so sorry." Elizabeth's voice softened. "I hadn't realised your mother had–"

"You misunderstood, Lady Elizabeth. She hasn't passed, she's quite alive – just preferred the theatrical life to domestic arrangements. Last we heard, she was touring with a theatre company in New York. It suited her temperament far better."

Another canvas slipped from Stacey's grasp. Elizabeth grabbed it. "Here, let us help you with those." She gathered two of the smaller canvases and handed them to Meli.

They followed Stacey into the gallery. Several paintings lined the white walls, while others waited in neat stacks against the baseboards. A wooden ladder stood beside an empty section of picture rail, a hammer and nails balanced on its top step.

"Just set them down here." Stacey indicated a space beneath the window. "I'll sort through them when–"

Raised voices from above cut through his words. Elizabeth glanced up at the ceiling as the argument intensified – two distinct voices, though their words were lost in the heat of the exchange.

A door slammed. One set of footsteps paced overhead while another struck against the external stairs. A stumble, then a sharp intake of breath, followed by a muttered curse.

A woman swept in, her shoulders rigid. At the sight of Elizabeth and Meli, she drew herself upright, chin lifting as her features settled into place.

"Is everything all right?" Stacey set down his canvases. "We couldn't help but overhear—"

"It was nothing. Just a minor difference of opinion." The woman's mouth tightened as she adjusted a frame that hung perfectly straight. "You know how temperamental these artistic types are." She turned from the wall, her smile too bright. "Aren't you going to introduce me to your friends?"

"Of course. Mrs Vivienne Marchant – Lady Elizabeth Hawthorne and her cousin, Miss Meli Diomaros."

"Delighted to meet you both, but I'm afraid I must dash – so much to do before the exhibition tonight. You'll be all right here on your own, won't you, Stacey?" She paused in the doorway, one hand resting on the frame. "And please call me Vivi," she said before disappearing through the doorway.

"I should get on." Stacey gestured to the stack of canvases leaning against the wall. "But thank you both for your help."

"Of course. Until tonight, then." Elizabeth and Meli made their way out into the June sunshine.

Meli glanced back at the gallery door. "Who do you suppose Mrs Marchant was arguing with? She seemed rather unsettled by it despite pretending otherwise."

"Probably something to do with the exhibition tonight. I would imagine everyone's nerves are frayed with all the preparations."

"I'm sure you're right." Meli tilted her head, her brow creasing. "Have you heard of this Jasper Vale Stacey mentioned?"

"I have indeed. He has quite a reputation in Brighton's art circles – and none of it good. I'll tell you all about him over a cup of tea."

"Look!" Meli caught Elizabeth's arm.

"What is it?"

"Over there, by that empty kiosk. Isn't that Essie? Shall we ask her to join us?"

Elizabeth followed Meli's gaze.

How peculiar – Essie had declined her invitation to join them on their walk, insisting she had boring errands to attend to.

But what errands could she possibly have on the pier?

Elizabeth shifted position, trying to glimpse through the clusters of holidaymakers obscuring her view.

And who was that man she was with?

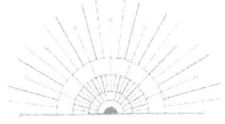

Chapter Four

ANYONE WHO WAS ANYONE in the Brighton art scene had gathered at the Palace Pier Exhibition Rooms. This was Jasper Vale's first exhibition in over a decade, and art critics and society columnists crowded the gallery, eager to witness his return. The sale of his painting *Tuscan Spring* to renowned art collector and philanthropist Sir Geoffrey Ward for fifty guineas had sparked fresh interest in the artist's work.

Waiters threaded through the crowd, silver trays of champagne balanced high. In his corner, Stacey's canvases drew the eye – fragments of seaside life captured in bold strokes and bright colours. A girl's skirts swirled as she chased a hoop past candy-striped beach huts, friends shared ice creams outside the Pavilion

Gardens, their laughter visible in every sweep of his brush.

Vivi Marchant charmed her way through the exhibition, a ripple of laughter following in her wake. Her sea-foam silk dress shimmered beneath the electric lights, her platinum hair a perfect arrangement of finger waves beneath a crystal-studded bandeau.

Near the far wall, beneath a draped canvas, Jasper Vale commanded attention. His once-striking features had sharpened with age, his dark jacket hanging loose on his frame. A cigarette dangled from his fingers, ash dropping unnoticed onto the polished floor as he gestured to his hidden masterpiece.

"I suppose I ought to say hello." Gigi's voice carried a weight Elizabeth rarely heard. "He's stayed at the villa several times, so I can hardly ignore him." She turned to Essie. "Coming?"

Essie's fingers tightened around her clutch. "No, I'll wait here."

Elizabeth watched Gigi navigate the crowd towards Vale. He paused mid-sentence, his face brightening as he caught sight of her. His hands spread wide in welcome as he bent to brush her cheek with a kiss. As they spoke, Gigi gestured towards Elizabeth and the others. His eyes locked with Essie's, his lips twisting into a smirk that held no warmth.

Essie plucked a champagne flute from a passing waiter's tray and drank deep, her throat working as she swallowed half the glass in one go.

Meli turned to her. "Do you know Jasper Vale?"

"Not really, I've met him a handful of times at the villa in Tuscany." Essie drained her glass and set it on a passing tray.

How peculiar. Gigi had painted quite a different picture at breakfast. According to her cousin, Vale, captivated from the moment he saw Essie, had refused all other models. Yet Essie spoke as if she barely knew him.

Gigi slipped back into their circle. "Rosalind and the others are taking their time. Tommy promised they wouldn't be late."

The gallery doors opened, and Gigi's shoulders slumped. "Oh, it's just Stacey's father."

Sir Lionel Grimwald entered, silver-haired and straight-backed, acknowledging greetings with the merest nod of his head.

They watched as Stacey walked his father through his collection, Sir Lionel studying each of them with judicial detachment.

"Poor Stacey." Meli turned to the others. "Do you think we should rescue him?"

"You two go ahead." Gigi's gaze swept the gallery. "I've just spotted some friends I haven't seen in forever."

Elizabeth and Meli crossed to where Stacey's paintings hung along the far wall.

"Stacey, these are quite splendid," Meli said, studying the canvases. "I had no idea you were so talented. You're sure to sell them all."

"It's a pleasant enough hobby, Miss…?"

"Diomaros, Meli Diomaros."

Sir Lionel's expression tightened. "But hardly the foundation for a respectable future."

"Er, Father, let me introduce Lady Elizabeth Hawthorne – my father, Sir Lionel Grimwald."

"Hawthorne? Any relation to William Hawthorne, magistrate?"

"Yes, he's my brother. Do you know him?"

"I know *of* him, rather than know him personally. We may serve under the same system, but we interpret its duties rather differently."

"William believes everyone deserves a chance at redemption. His work with the youth reformatory has shown remarkable results."

Sir Lionel's brows drew down into a severe line. "I don't hold with these modern approaches to justice. Rules exist for a reason, Lady Elizabeth, and without proper consequences, without order, society would collapse."

He inclined his head to where Gigi stood with Essie and a cluster of Brighton's social set. "Heaven help us if young Pembroke gains a seat in the next election. Another idealist with dangerous liberal notions."

"Laurence Pembroke?" Elizabeth asked.

"Indeed. Running as a Liberal against Marshall Havers. Now there's a man who understands the proper order of things." Sir Lionel shook his head. "How Pembroke Senior will be able to show his face at the Carlton Club when he returns…"

So this was the mysterious Mr Laurence Pembroke. The same man she'd glimpsed with Essie on the pier earlier that morning, and the cause of that contretemps with Rosalind at The Lux. As she watched, a glance passed between Essie and Pembroke – subtle, but unmistakable. Perhaps Mrs Drummond-Ward and her society column had been right after all.

Elizabeth watched as Morton circled the edges of the gathering with his camera. Pembroke obscured his face with his hand before joining a cluster of guests near the window.

It was almost as if he was avoiding being photographed with Essie.

The gallery doors swung open. Rosalind barged in, Tommy and Sylvia trailing in her wake.

Elizabeth turned as Gigi and Essie headed them off. "Where on earth have you been?" Gigi kept her voice low.

"Ask Sylvia." Rosalind's lip curled. "Some of us have a job to do, *apparently*."

"I've said I'm sorry." Sylvia's fingers twisted at her sleeve. "The shop was–"

"Yes, yes, we know. The shop was busy."

"Can't you just let it go?" Tommy stepped between them. "She's already apologised ... more than once."

Gigi peered behind them. "Where's Markus?"

"Locked away with his precious manuscript. Anyone would think we're witnessing the birth of the next D.H. Lawrence classic." Rosalind caught the arm of a passing waiter, took a glass and emptied it before exchanging it for another.

Sir Lionel's shoulders stiffened, his lips pressing into a thin line.

Rosalind flicked a glance in Sir Lionel's direction before taking another sip from her glass. "Have we missed it?"

"Missed what?" Gigi asked.

"The great unveiling."

"I didn't know you were such an admirer of Vale's work." Gigi's brow creased.

"There's rather a lot you don't know about me."

"Ladies and gentlemen." The chime of crystal cut through the hum of conversation. "I won't keep you long, don't worry. I know you've come here for the art and not to–" Vivi's smile froze.

Elizabeth turned. At the back of the gallery, a man in a frayed tweed jacket and paint-spattered boots watched the proceedings.

"Er ... ladies and gentlemen." Vivi's shoulders straightened. "May I present ... Jasper Vale."

Vale stumbled against a display pedestal beside his canvas, catching himself on the edge. "Thank you, Vivi, always so..." He blinked, seeming to lose his thread. "Where was I? Ah yes. This piece is part of a series I've been working on for ... well, it's a long time, I know that much. Several collectors have shown interest, but one seems ... determined to acquire the entire collection."

The glass slid from Essie's grasp, champagne spraying the front of her dress before the crystal splintered at her feet.

"I'd better ... before it dries." Essie disappeared through the crowd.

Elizabeth caught the tightness around Pembroke's mouth as he tracked Essie's retreat.

"And now..." Vale's fingers closed around the fabric. He pulled, letting it fall. "I give you *Nymphaeum*."

A collective intake of breath filled the gallery.

On the canvas, Rosalind reclined against silk cushions, a length of fine chiffon draped across her modesty.

Rosalind lifted her glass in a toast to Vale, the corner of her mouth curving upward.

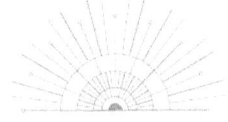

Chapter Five

THE COLLECTIVE GASP FRACTURED into whispers and shocked glances, while Rosalind stood before her painted self, lips curved in satisfaction as cameras flashed.

Vale stumbled against a display pedestal, sending a small bronze sculpture wobbling. Elizabeth watched him try to right it, his fingers clumsy as the sculpture hit the floor with a dull thud.

Vivi's eyes darted between Vale and the paint-splattered stranger as she propelled him out the door before crossing to Vale's side. She linked her arm through his. "He hasn't been right for days, you know. A touch of summer flu." Her smile stretched thin. "But you know Jasper … the show must go on." She summoned the waiting staff. "Help yourselves to champagne, there's plenty to go around." Taking Vale's arm more firmly, she steered him towards the gallery's side door, his uneven steps echoing on the wooden stairs as she led him up to the studio above.

"Summer flu, my eye," came a voice from the crowd. "Is that what we're calling it these days?"

Her companion shook his head. "Such a waste. He could have been one of the greats if it hadn't been for the drink."

"That, and his sheer bloody-mindedness," came the dry observation somewhere to Elizabeth's left.

"People like Vale represent everything that plagues modern society." Sir Lionel stood with the rigid posture that served him well in court. "This endless appetite for excess. We see it everywhere now – a complete disregard for propriety and moral restraint."

"Some believe it's circumstances and social conditions that shape behaviour rather than the other way around." Elizabeth set her champagne glass on a nearby table.

"Social conditions?" Sir Lionel's shoulders stiffened. "Next, you'll suggest we excuse every thief and wastrel who claims poverty as justification. A dangerous path, Lady Elizabeth. These new notions of reform and rehabilitation … mere fashion, like women's votes and shortened hemlines."

"The evidence suggests otherwise. In Manchester, where they've implemented reform programmes in the prison system, re-offending rates have fallen by nearly half."

"No doubt your brother has been filling your head with this progressive nonsense?" The words caught in Sir Lionel's throat as a coughing fit took hold, his hand batting away Stacey's proffered champagne glass before composing himself. "Heaven preserve us when idealists mistake coddling for justice. Brighton was once a respectable town. But now we have women parading half-dressed on the beach, and politicians promising paradise to the undeserving."

"Contrary to what some believe, women are quite capable of forming their own opinions without male guidance."

Rosalind plucked a fresh glass of champagne from a passing tray and lifted it in toast. "I'll drink to that."

"You're young yet. Experience and, perhaps marriage, will teach you that social order demands a firm hand." Sir Lionel's eyes narrowed in Rosalind's direction. "Too much indulgence and the whole system unravels. Already decent people fear to walk certain streets after dark."

"Perhaps because we've relied too long on punishment alone. The Howard League's study of the Birmingham prison reforms shows that education and employment opportunities reduce crime more effectively than–"

"The Howard League." Sir Lionel's eyes rolled skyward. "A collection of bleeding hearts who'd turn our prisons into holiday camps. Next, you'll tell me we should invite criminals for afternoon tea. When you've sat on the bench as long as I have, and seen the worst of humanity parade before you on an almost weekly basis, then perhaps you'll understand the importance of maintaining order in a civilised society."

Elizabeth held her tongue. Experience had taught her that men like Sir Lionel viewed statistics and research as mere inconveniences when they challenged their long-held convictions.

"More champagne, anyone?" Rosalind grinned over the rim of her glass. "Ah, Vivi." She caught Vivi's arm as she re-entered the gallery. "Tell us, how is the great master? Although knowing Vale, I wouldn't be surprised if he'd staged the whole thing just for attention. We all know how he hates to share the spotlight, isn't that right, Vivi?"

"You know how these artistic types are." Vivi replied. "But I suppose Vale is a little more conceited than most."

Elizabeth recalled the Vale painting purchased by Sir Geoffrey Ward last month for fifty guineas. The newspapers and art journals had been filled with it, while critics praised its precise lines and refined composition – so unlike the wild sweeps of colour and raw emotional style that had made Vale's name. *An artist reborn*, they'd claimed.

"I suppose you'd know better than most." Rosalind angled her champagne glass, studying Vivi over its rim.

"Sorry?"

"Well, according to Vale, you two were something of an item back in your Gaiety Girl days?"

"Vale's memory isn't what it was." Vivi shifted her weight, her gaze catching Sir Lionel's eye before darting away. "I wouldn't set too much store by what he says. If you'll excuse me."

Elizabeth touched Vivi's sleeve. "How is Mr Vale?"

"He's resting in the attic studio." Vivi glanced at her wristwatch, her lips thinning. "But he'll rejoin us a little later, when he's feeling better."

Over Vivi's shoulder, Elizabeth spotted Pembroke easing in through the side door. He kept close to the wall, smoothing his dark hair before lifting a glass of champagne from a passing waiter, his movements too deliberate to be casual.

Elizabeth caught Gigi's eye. "Has Essie returned yet?"

"She hasn't, come to think of it." A small frown crossed Gigi's brow.

"Interesting choice of perspective, wouldn't you say, Stacey?" Tommy studied the portrait, head tilted in exaggerated contemplation. "I daresay one might even call it ... perky."

"All au naturel, darling." Rosalind slanted a look at Tommy from beneath dark lashes.

The lines deepened between Sir Lionel's brows as he turned away. "I'll bid you good evening."

"Why don't you stay a little longer, Father? You've barely had a chance to view any of the other works?"

"That ring you're wearing." Sylvia took a half-step towards the canvas, narrowing her eyes as she studied the portrait. "It's rather striking, isn't it?"

"Striking?" Rosalind's fingers brushed the pearls at her throat as she faced Sylvia. "Don't you mean ghastly? All those little enamel flowers and discoloured seed pearls – it's like something from a Christmas cracker, rather than Asprey's. And that stone is the most hideous shade of green – it reminds me of cheap absinthe."

"If you disliked it that much, why did you wear it?" Gigi asked.

"Because Vale insisted. You don't think I wore it by choice, do you? For an artist, you'd expect him to have a better sense of aesthetics."

"Trust me, I don't think anyone's looking at the ring." Tommy rocked back on his heels, the corner of his mouth twitching as his gaze flicked between Sir Lionel, hunched over the painting, and his son's obvious discomfort. "Then again … I could be wrong."

"Father, Aldridge's Sussex landscapes are just over there. Perhaps you'd like to…"

"I think your father's quite happy where he is." A smile tugged at the corners of Tommy's mouth.

"This ring." Sir Lionel turned on his heel to face Rosalind. "Do you have it?"

"Of course I don't have it. What on earth would I want with that old thing?"

"Do you know where it is?" Sir Lionel's gaze fixed on Rosalind.

"How should I know? Why don't you ask Vale?" Her eyes widened as she stepped back. "Or Vivi over there, Vale always claimed the ring had sentimental value."

Sir Lionel's gaze slid to where Vivi gestured at one of the seascapes, Pembroke nodding as she traced the curve of a wave in the air.

"Now's your chance," Rosalind murmured into her champagne as Vivi steered Pembroke towards Stacey's paintings.

"I'll take my leave, son. I have some briefs to review before morning."

"Very well, I'll walk you out."

"No need, you stay here with your *friends*." Sir Lionel nodded as he turned towards the door. "Pembroke."

"Sir Lionel."

The tension ebbed from their small group as Sir Lionel made his way across the gallery. Elizabeth watched the door click shut behind him, her mind turning over Sir Lionel's peculiar interest in Vale's painting. The way he'd scrutinised it at such close quarters had been odd indeed, particularly since his fascination seemed to have nothing to do with Rosalind's artistic merits, and everything to do with that ring.

"Mr Pembroke, let me show you these by an up-and-coming young artist, Stacey Ellis." Vivi winked at Stacey.

"Stacey and I are already acquainted." Pembroke studied the signature on the canvas before turning to Stacey. "But I had no idea you and the artist Stacey Ellis were one and the same."

Vivi's dark eyes held Stacey's for a moment, her fingers resting briefly on his arm.

"Wouldn't you prefer something a bit more … stimulating than seascapes, Pembroke?" Tommy's gaze flicked to Rosalind's portrait.

"Rumour has it, Laurence's tastes are a little more provincial these days." Rosalind said.

"While I, myself appreciate an artistic undressing, my father's tastes are rather more traditional."

"Ah, so it's a gift for an older gentleman?" Vivi asked.

"A birthday present. He and my mother return from the Cape in a few days."

A dull thud echoed overhead.

Vivi startled. "I'd, er … I'd better check on Jasper."

"What do you suppose has happened?" Meli tilted her head toward the ceiling.

"Knowing Vale, he's most likely fallen off a chair, drunk." Gigi rolled her eyes. "It wouldn't be the first time. One time when he was staying with us in Tuscany, Mama thought he'd killed himself when he fell from the first-floor veranda."

"Was he hurt?" Meli's eyes widened.

"No, luckily a couple of oleanders broke his fall."

Gigi tilted her head, studying the portrait. "Rosalind, I have to ask. Whatever made you agree to … this?"

"Why not?" Rosalind's smile held a challenge.

"Well." Tommy's grin widened. "I hope he paid you handsomely."

"There's more to life than money." Rosalind held up her champagne glass, studying the light through the bubbles. "Better to be talked about than sink into obscurity like some dreary little housewife."

Sylvia's cheeks flushed pink, her gaze dropping to the floor.

Vivi appeared at Pembroke's elbow, the rouge on her cheeks stark against her pallor. "Mr Pembroke, would you mind accompanying me upstairs? There's been something of an ... accident."

Elizabeth caught an edge in Vivi's voice. "Forgive me." She took a step closer. "I couldn't help overhearing, but I've some experience in these situations."

Vivi's gaze flickered between them.

Pembroke's chin lowered slightly, his eyes locked on Vivi. "Whatever's the matter?"

"You'd better come with me..." Her fingers pressed against her collarbone. "Both of you."

Elizabeth caught Gigi's eye. Her cousin's brows lifted, and she gave a small shake of the head in reply, before falling into step with Vivi and Pembroke as they left the gallery.

"It's up here." Vivi turned on the wooden stair. "But mind the step there; it's loose."

At the top, Vivi paused, her hands twisting together. "Lady Elizabeth, I think it would be better if Mr Pembroke went first ... there's a lot of blood."

"Perhaps Mrs Marchant's right."

"I appreciate your concern." Elizabeth tilted her chin. "But I can assure you that whatever is waiting behind that door, I've seen worse."

"As you wish." Vivi backed away from the door. "I'll wait here."

Pembroke pushed open the door and stepped inside; Elizabeth was close on his heels. Turpentine and old paint filled the air, sharp and acrid.

Moonlight slanted through the sash window, illuminating Essie, frozen beside the easel, her eyes wide and unseeing.

The palette knife trembled in her grip, its blade slick with blood.

At her feet lay Jasper Vale's crumpled body.

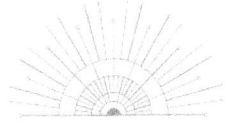

Chapter Six

MOONLIGHT SPILLED THROUGH THE studio window, catching the palette knife in Essie's hand – its blade slick with blood. Elizabeth's gaze moved from Vale's still form on the paint-spattered boards to his outstretched arm, fingers curled against the air. A wooden chair lay overturned beside him, his head fallen against his shoulder, while Essie remained frozen.

Pembroke dropped to one knee, pressing two fingers against Vale's neck. He met Elizabeth's eyes and shook his head.

"Essie." Elizabeth kept her voice low as she edged closer.

Essie pressed against the wall, her eyes wide and unfocused, her chest rising and falling in quick, shallow breaths.

The palette knife slipped from her fingers, clattering against the floorboards.

"I should fetch the police." Pembroke rose, the lines around his mouth deepening. "Would you mind staying with her?"

Elizabeth nodded as Pembroke brushed past her, pausing at the top of the stairs to speak with Vivi.

"Elizabeth?" Meli rushed in. "I came to see if everything was–" Her words died. "Is that ... Vale on the floor?"

"Yes."

Meli's gaze shifted to Essie. "Why is Essie here?"

Elizabeth dipped her head closer to Meli's ear. "Did you speak to Pembroke?"

"I passed him and Vivi on the stairs, but they seemed in rather a hurry." Meli's gaze slid to Essie. "Do you know what happened?"

"She hasn't said a word since we arrived." Elizabeth shook her head, squinting against the dimness as her gaze flicked over the studio.

"Can you stay with her? I'll see if I can find her something for the shock."

Meli nodded, slipping an arm around Essie's shoulders. She guided Essie to a wooden stool at the far end.

Elizabeth surveyed the cramped studio, settling on a cluttered workbench where an oil lamp nestled between paint-crusted brushes and stained rags.

She struck a match from a box on the bench, touching it to the lamp's wick and adjusting the flame. Amber and green glass bottles caught the lamplight – some whisky, others gin, their contents at varying levels.

Elizabeth lifted the first bottle, uncorking it with care. The acrid smell of turpentine stung her nose. She replaced it and reached for another, this one square-shaped with a worn label. The cork came free with a soft pop. The sharp bite of spirits met her nose, but underneath lay an odd, earthy undertone that made her pause. Moving on, she selected a third bottle. This smelled cleaner – brandy, perhaps?

A chipped enamel mug lay on its side among the tubes of paint. Elizabeth righted it, frowning at the residue inside. She poured a measure of brandy into the mug, swirled it around, then emptied it into an upturned jam jar nearby, before pouring a fresh measure and carrying it back to Essie.

"Here." Elizabeth pressed the mug into Essie's trembling hands. "For the shock."

A thump and clatter sounded from below, followed by a muffled oath and hurried footsteps pounding up the wooden staircase. A young constable burst through the doorway, his helmet slightly askew. His face blanched as his eyes darted from Vale's lifeless form to the dark pool spreading across the floorboards.

"I ... er ..." He shifted his weight from foot to foot. "I..."

"Constable. As you can see, there's been an ... incident, of a most serious nature." Elizabeth gestured towards Vale. "So, I suggest you notify your Chief Inspector immediately."

"Yes, miss. Of course, miss." He backed towards the door, his eyes darting between Elizabeth and Vale. "But don't you go touching anything while I'm gone."

The constable spun on his heel and fled, stumbling on the last few treads.

Elizabeth paced the confined space, oil lamp in hand. The weak light barely reached the corners of the studio, making any proper examination impossible. The palette knife lay where Essie had dropped it – what if someone stood on it and damaged it?

She retrieved a cotton handkerchief from her bag and crouched beside the fallen palette knife. Using her thumb and forefinger beneath the handkerchief, she lifted it without touching the blood-stained blade, then set it on top of the fabric on the workbench.

Meli glanced at the doorway. "Should I take her home? She's shaking."

"Better wait for the Chief Inspector. He'll probably want to speak with her."

"I..." Essie's hands tightened around the mug. She lifted it to her lips, taking a small sip, wincing as the amber liquid hit the back of her throat. "He was..."

A police klaxon wailed in the distance, growing louder as it drew nearer. Essie froze, her eyes wide as they found first Meli, then Elizabeth.

"Try not to worry." Elizabeth chose her words carefully. "Just tell the Chief Inspector what happened."

Stair treads creaked and groaned as someone approached. "Chief Inspector's on his way up, miss."

Seconds later, several pairs of boot heels struck the wooden steps in quick succession. "Mind that second step!" the young constable called down. A stumble and muffled curse suggested the warning came too late.

The Chief Inspector marched in, his ruddy face surveying the scene. Three constables followed in his wake, crowding the cramped space behind their superior's broad shoulders. One stumbled, knocking into his back. The Chief Inspector turned, thick eyebrows drawing together, nostrils flaring as he turned to them.

"Sir, I…" The constable's mouth opened and closed. His gaze darted between the women and his superior. "When I arrived, they were… that is to say…"

"You must forgive the constable," Elizabeth said, taking pity on the young man. "He was so intent on notifying you he didn't have time to take our names even, but he knew this warranted your personal attention, Chief Inspector."

The Chief Inspector's gaze shifted from the stammering constable to Elizabeth, his expression doubtful. "And you are?"

"*Lady* Elizabeth Hawthorne." She met his gaze steadily.

"I see." His thumbs hooked beneath his lapels as he drew himself up. "And what exactly are you doing here?"

"Well, Mrs Marchant–"

The Chief Inspector held up his palm to her. "Peters, check if he's dead."

One of the constables crouched beside Vale's body, pressing two fingers against his neck. "Dead, sir."

"Do we know who it is?"

"Jasper Vale, sir."

A grunt escaped the Chief Inspector's throat. "Can't say I'm surprised." He turned back to Elizabeth. "So, you mentioned Mrs Marchant … Isn't there any more light here?"

Elizabeth's jaw tightened as she caught Meli's eye. "I'm afraid this is all we have." She indicated the oil lamp.

"Did any of you see what happened?"

Elizabeth hesitated, her gaze sliding to Essie. "Miss Baker…"

"Right. Everyone out, except Miss Baker."

"But she's in shock." Elizabeth stepped closer to Essie. "Someone should stay with her."

"This isn't a tea party, Lady Elizabeth. Out. All of you."

Elizabeth crouched before Essie, her hand light on the other woman's arm. "Just tell them what happened."

At the doorway, Elizabeth paused. "Chief Inspector? I should mention I moved the palette knife to the workbench."

"You did what?"

"The murder weapon … I was concerned someone might damage it."

"Why, of all the…" His face darkened. "I suggest you leave now before I charge you with tampering with evidence."

Meli glanced back towards the studio as they descended the steps. "I hate to leave her there alone. Do you think she'll be all right?"

"It's not as if the Chief Inspector gave us any choice in the matter."

"You don't think she's guilty, do you?"

"Mind the second step." Elizabeth steadied Meli's elbow, the question churning over in her mind.

Only that morning Gigi had told her over breakfast that once Vale had set eyes on Essie, he'd refused to use any other model – yet Essie claimed she barely knew him.

Then there was Essie's disappearance moments after Vale announced his buyer for the full *Nymphaeum* series, only for her to reappear in the attic studio standing over Vale's lifeless form while clutching the murder weapon in her hand.

Elizabeth wanted to believe in Essie's innocence, but so many pieces of the puzzle that was Miss Essie Baker, refused to fit together.

Chapter Seven

ELIZABETH HESITATED ON THE final step, Meli's question still turning in her mind.

Did she believe Essie was guilty?

Her thoughts returned to their first encounter at Brighton Station just yesterday, and despite what she'd just seen, she found it almost impossible to believe her cousin's best friend was a murderer.

Yet ... there was the question of the bloodied palette knife clutched in her hand, her insistence she barely knew Vale despite their obvious history, and her reaction to Vale's announcement about the *Nymphaeum* series.

None of it made sense.

"Elizabeth?" Meli prompted.

"I, er–"

"If you'd be so kind, miss." A police constable stepped out of the shadows. "Everyone's to wait inside the gallery until questioned. Chief Inspector's orders, miss."

Elizabeth inclined her head. "Of course."

The constable rapped twice on the gallery entrance.

A face peered around the edge of the door. "A couple of stragglers for you, Thompson."

Thompson stepped aside, swinging the door wider, allowing Elizabeth and Meli admittance before positioning himself against the doorframe.

Gigi rushed to Elizabeth's side. "What on earth is happening?" Her gaze darted between Elizabeth and Meli. "Where's Essie?"

Elizabeth's gaze swept the gallery. Vivi sat alone in a corner, a glass of amber liquid trembling in her hand. "Hasn't Vivi said anything? Or Pembroke?"

"Vivi hasn't said a word." Gigi shook her head. "And no one's seen hide nor hair of Pembroke since he left with you and Vivi."

Had the would-be MP fled at the first hint of scandal to preserve his precious political campaign?

She pressed close to her cousin's ear; her words meant for Gigi alone.

Gigi's face paled, her eyes wide. "I should go to her–"

"I'm not sure the Chief Inspector will allow it. He all but turfed Meli and I out on our ear."

"Chief Inspector Walsh acts as if Brighton's morality rests entirely on his shoulders. He's just being ridiculous … Essie wouldn't harm a fly."

Raised voices near the entrance drew their attention to where Rosalind stood before the police constable guarding the entrance, her shoulders rigid with indignation.

"This is utterly barbaric." Rosalind's voice carried across the gallery. "You can't expect to keep us here indefinitely, like common criminals. I have dinner plans."

The constable shifted his weight. "No one leaves until Chief Inspector Walsh says so, miss."

"Oh, for heaven's sake." Rosalind rummaged through her evening bag and withdrew a silver cigarette case. "Couldn't I just step outside for a cigarette then?"

"Sorry, miss. Chief Inspector's orders."

"What exactly do you think I'm going to do – make a dash for it?" Rosalind tilted her head to the side. "I'm the Honourable Rosalind Delacourt of twenty-three Lewes Crescent. There. Now you know where to find me should I run off."

The constable stood firm, arms folded. "Orders is orders, miss."

"Oh, heavens." Gigi touched Elizabeth's arm. "I'd better fetch Rosalind before she's arrested." She crossed to where Rosalind stared down the constable, linking her arm through Rosalind's. "Rosalind," Gigi ground out through clenched teeth. "Everyone's looking."

"Let them look; I don't care." Rosalind yanked her arm free. "I, for one, am fed up with being cooped up here like we're criminals or something."

"Why don't we rejoin the others so Elizabeth can fill you in."

Rosalind glanced over her shoulder, eyes narrowing at Elizabeth as they made their way over.

"Does anyone know what's going on?" Sylvia twisted her gold locket between her fingers. "Why are the police here?"

"Elizabeth is about to enlighten us, apparently." Rosalind arched a brow.

Elizabeth recounted what she'd witnessed in the attic studio.

Tommy's brows shot up. "You don't think Essie did it, do you?"

"How can you even ask such a thing?" Gigi's eyes flashed. "Of course she didn't."

Sylvia swayed, her shoulder brushing Tommy's arm.

"Stacey, fetch that chair." Tommy steadied Sylvia's elbow. "Here." He guided her hand to his untouched champagne.

Rosalind slid a cigarette into her holder, watching Tommy hover over Sylvia. She lifted it to her lips, drawing on the unlit cigarette.

"Madam, smoking isn't permitted–" A waiter stepped forward.

"It's not even lit." Rosalind thrust the holder towards his face. "Or do you need spectacles?"

"How much longer are we going to be held hostage like this?" A grey-haired man approached Constable Thomson at the entrance.

"Just waiting on the Chief Inspector, Lord Abbott, sir ."

Constable Thomson leapt aside as Chief Inspector Walsh barrelled through the front entrance, flanked by several officers.

"What's the meaning of this, Walsh?" Lord Abbott approached the Chief Inspector. "How much longer are we to be held here against our will?"

"There's been a death, my Lord."

A wave of murmurs swept through the gallery.

"Murder?" Lord Abbott's voice rose above the murmurs. "Is that why we're being detained? You believe the killer is here among us?"

Elizabeth's attention drifted to where Vivi stood, the crystal tumbler trembling in her grip as she tilted back her head and drained its contents.

"No, my Lord. We have a suspect."

"Then, I insist you let us leave this instant."

"Of course, my Lord." Walsh's expression hardened. "Constable Morris will take your party's details, and we'll arrange to collect statements from everyone."

"Well, they'd better get a move on, man. I have supper reservations at the Grand."

The Chief Inspector's eyes narrowed. "Constable, attend to his Lordship, will you?"

He threaded his way between the guests toward the constable taking Gigi's details. "No one's to leave Brighton, do you hear? We'll need formal statements from all of you."

"Sir Lionel Grimwald was here earlier." Rosalind toyed with her cigarette holder. "Won't you be requiring *his* details?"

"I hardly think that will be necessary, young lady." His attention caught on Rosalind's portrait, heat rising beneath his starched collar. "Should I need to speak to his Lordship, I need look no further than his chambers at the Royal Courts of Justice."

"What about Essie?" Gigi took a half-step forward. "Can we take her home now?"

"I'm afraid not, Miss Hamilton-Smythe." The Chief Inspector's expression hardened. "She's on her way to the station, where she'll be charged with the murder of Jasper Vale."

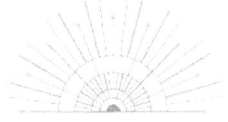

Chapter Eight

ELIZABETH'S SHOULDERS SAGGED AGAINST the wooden window recess of the sitting-room, her head resting against the frame. An abandoned teacup sat on the side table, the liquid long since grown cold in the quiet hours before sunrise.

Beyond the glass, she watched a ginger tomcat slink across the communal gardens of Adelaide Crescent, muscles tensed beneath his russet fur as he stalked some invisible prey through the flower beds.

Behind her, Meli lay curled into the corner of the sage green damask sofa, while Gigi had finally succumbed to exhaustion in the matching armchair after hours of waiting by the telephone for news of Essie.

Elizabeth's thoughts drifted from the garden to the events at the Palace Pier Exhibition Rooms the previous evening. The image of Essie standing over Vale's body, the bloodied palette knife clutched in her hand, rose unbidden in Elizabeth's mind. The Chief Inspector's words still rang in her ears. *She's on her way to the station, where she'll be charged with the murder of Jasper Vale.*

The purr of an engine drew Elizabeth's attention as a dark blue Silver Ghost approached Adelaide Crescent. She shifted position in the window recess as the motorcar slowed outside one of Gigi's neighbour's houses. Through the motorcar window, Essie's face came into view in the back seat, then a man beside her leaned forward. Elizabeth pressed closer, squinting. Could that be Pembroke?

Essie turned to her companion, brushing a light kiss against his cheek before alighting from the motorcar. She lifted her hand in farewell as the Silver Ghost pulled away from the kerb, then hurried through the communal gardens towards the house.

Gigi startled awake at the sound of a key turning in the front door. Meli pushed herself up from the sofa cushions as Elizabeth turned from the window. Essie appeared in the doorway, her face drawn and pale, exhaustion etched in the dark circles beneath her eyes.

"Essie!" Gigi flew across the room, enveloping her friend in an embrace. "Why didn't you telephone? I would have collected you rather than letting you take a taxi."

"I didn't take a taxi." Elizabeth noticed the quick exchange of glances between Essie and Gigi. "My ... solicitor brought me home."

"I knew that pompous Chief Inspector Walsh would soon realise his mistake and release you–"

"No, you've misunderstood. I haven't been cleared. I've been released on bail pending further investigation."

"I don't understand." Gigi perched on the arm of Essie's chair. "Not cleared but released? What does that mean exactly?"

"I'm not too sure myself." Essie sank deeper into the chair. "I'm just grateful to be out of those police cells."

"It means the magistrate released her, but Essie must present herself at the next hearing," Elizabeth explained.

Meli's eyes widened. "You went before a magistrate?"

Essie shook her head. "My solicitor handled everything. He's even arranged with the Chief Constable to keep my name out of the papers."

Elizabeth knew you needed a name with pull to rouse the Chief Constable, not a solicitor's letterhead; a name like Laurence Pembroke.

Mrs Bramley entered with a silver tea tray. "Mr Bramley noticed you were back when he was tending the roses, so I made a fresh pot. Thought you could all do with it after the night you've had." Her eyes darted from one to the other before settling on Essie. "You poor dear, you look done in. Let me make you a proper breakfast – some eggs and bacon, perhaps a couple of sausages? That'll soon put the roses back in your cheeks."

"Not for me, thank you, Mrs Bramley." Essie pressed her fingers to her temple. "Just a nice cup of tea, then bed."

"A slice of toast, at least. And a soft-boiled egg?" Mrs Bramley remained by the tea tray, unwilling to admit defeat. "You've had nothing since dinner yesterday, I'll wager."

"The tea will be perfect, thank you." Essie's words dissolved into a stifled yawn.

"Very well." Mrs Bramley gave a small shake of her head as she moved towards the door. "But if you change your minds, I can make up something for you in a jiffy." She pulled the door shut behind her.

"Elizabeth can help you, Essie." Gigi started towards the tea tray. "She's solved several murders already. If anyone can find out who killed Vale, she can."

"I'll see to the tea." Meli rose from the sofa. "You stay with Essie."

Elizabeth shifted in her chair. "I appreciate your faith in me, Gigi, but this is rather different. And I can only help if–" She paused, choosing her words with care. "If I have all the facts. Every detail matters, especially in a murder investigation."

Gigi placed a reassuring hand on her friend's shoulder. "Elizabeth won't judge, will you?"

"Of course not, but if I'm to help you, I'll need the truth. All of it."

Essie took the teacup from Meli, the saucer resting on her knees. "Vale was blackmailing me over a painting from my time in Tuscany. I had just lost my job and was working as an artist's model to make ends meet."

"This painting, was it part of the *Nymphaeum* series? Like Rosalind's?"

A flush crept across Essie's cheeks. "Yes, though mine isn't nearly as … revealing as Rosalind's."

"What exactly is this *Nymphaeum*?" Elizabeth asked.

"It's something Vale began working on years ago, when he was still relatively unknown. He said he was fascinated by women as figures of contradiction – desirable but untouchable." Essie set the teacup back on its saucer. "He claimed he wanted to blur the line between worship and objectification."

"No wonder you reacted the way you did when Vale said he had a buyer for the whole series." Elizabeth said.

"He'd promised it was for his own personal collection and he'd never part with it for any amount of money." Essie stared into her teacup. "I just can't bear the thought of anyone else seeing it – someone who might recognise me. That's why I went to his studio last night. To plead with him. But when I got there, he was slumped over in a chair, making these awful moaning sounds. I assumed he was just drunk as usual, but his head lolled forward and he let out this awful groan, so I reached for his shoulder to check if he was all right, but the moment I touched him he rolled off the chair onto the floor. Something dropped from his hand as he fell … I don't know what I was thinking, but I picked it up, and that's when…"

"That's when Vivi saw you?" Elizabeth asked.

Essie nodded, her fingers whitening against the teacup.

"But I still don't understand what Vale hoped to gain from blackmailing you?" Elizabeth's brow creased. "Forgive me, but you don't strike me as someone with access to large sums of money."

"I'm not."

Elizabeth studied Essie's down-turned face. Something still didn't add up. The Chief Constable's involvement, Pembroke's presence, Vale's blackmail of someone without means – none of it made sense.

"I think perhaps I should rest for a while." Essie pushed herself up from the chair, setting her cup and saucer down on the side table. "If you'll excuse me."

Elizabeth watched Essie leave, questions tumbling through her mind.

Why had Essie lied about Pembroke being in the motorcar? The kiss on his cheek suggested more than a casual relationship, yet here they were, sneaking around in the shadows like star-crossed lovers.

And Pembroke's position would certainly give him the connections needed to arrange Essie's release.

Then there was the sale of the *Nymphaeum* series. No wonder Essie had reacted as she had when Vale mentioned a buyer for the collection. Her portrait would belong to a stranger, beyond her control, available for anyone to view.

Unlike Rosalind, who seemed to revel in the scandal her portrait created, Essie had everything to lose. But why would Vale attempt to blackmail someone without means?

What could he possibly hope to gain?

Elizabeth turned Essie's story over in her mind, but she couldn't shake that nagging feeling that Essie still wasn't telling her everything.

But that didn't necessarily make her a murderer ... did it?

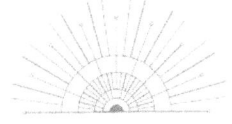

Chapter Nine

THE NINTH CHIME OF Hove Town Hall drifted through the bedroom window on the salt breeze, marking almost three hours since Essie's return from the police station. Beyond the glass, Elizabeth watched a couple of seagulls wheel against the cloudless sky, their wild circles matching the jumble of questions churning in her mind.

"I can hear your mind turning over from here."

"I need to see inside Vale's studio again." Elizabeth swung her legs over the side of the bed. "There was too much confusion last night, not to mention it was so dark you could barely see your hand in front of your face."

"Now?" Meli pushed herself up onto her elbow, dark curls falling around her shoulders.

"There's no time like the present." Elizabeth crossed to the privacy screen. "And Gigi said we could borrow her motorcar."

"As long as you're driving and not Gigi."

Meli slid from her bed, tugging open the wardrobe door and running her fingers along the hanging dresses.

"Could you pass me the lavender dress? The one with the pleated skirt."

She found Elizabeth's dress, then pulled out a drop-waist periwinkle blue day-dress with a white organdie collar for herself.

"Do you think the police will even let us near the studio?" Meli passed the lavender dress around the screen.

"Not if Chief Inspector Walsh has anything to do with it." Elizabeth's voice drifted from behind the screen. "But there's more than one way to crack a nut."

Meli settled on the padded stool at the dressing table, gathering her dark curls, pinning and tucking until her usual faux bob fell into place. She leaned closer to the triptych mirror, swiping on a coat of her soft pink lipstick.

Elizabeth crossed to her bed, perching on the corner as she fastened the silver buckles on her cream leather T-straps. Rising, she reached for her silver-backed brush, smoothing her inky dark bob into place.

With a final glance in the mirror, they collected their bags, and Elizabeth pulled the bedroom door shut behind them. At the top of the stairs, Lily, one of the housemaids, balanced on the third step, her slight frame stretching upward to dust the photo frames lining the wall.

"Good morning, my ladies." Lily's feather duster stilled as she made way for them to pass.

"Good morning, Lily," Elizabeth and Meli returned her greeting.

"Maudie, look at all these fingerprints on the silver." Mrs Bramley's voice drifted up the stairs. "This won't do at all; you'll have to do it again ... properly this time."

Mrs Bramley emerged from the kitchen, her eyebrows rising at the sight of Elizabeth and Meli. "I didn't expect to see any of you young ladies up this side of lunch, not after such a late night."

"We couldn't sleep." Meli replied.

"Off out, are you?" Mrs Bramley's gaze swept over their outfits.

"Er, yes." Elizabeth avoided her eye. "We have some errands to run."

"At least let me make you a spot of breakfast before you go; some tea and toast, perhaps?"

"Please don't trouble yourself, Mrs Bramley, we'll have something while we're out."

Mrs Bramley's lips thinned, her disapproval evident.

"Gigi said we could borrow her motorcar." Elizabeth kept her voice light. "Do you know where we might find the keys?"

"In the brass bowl on the mahogany hall table."

"Thank you." Elizabeth collected the keys as she and Meli made their way to the garage.

Elizabeth backed the carmine Vauxhall through the timber doors and along the gravel drive. She followed the curve of Adelaide Crescent, then turned onto Kings Road, where holidaymakers strolled along the seafront.

She parked the motorcar near the pier entrance. A boy in a blue cap raced past with a half-eaten toffee apple, while vendors arranged displays of rock candy and ginger beer beneath their striped awnings. Elizabeth and Meli walked the wooden boards past fortune tellers shuffling their cards and children feeding pennies into slot machines, until they reached Vivi's gallery.

Elizabeth recognised the young constable standing guard at the top of the studio steps, the same one who'd been the first to arrive at the scene the previous evening. His collar had wilted in the morning heat, and his face glowed pink beneath his helmet, while sweat darkened the heavy wool of his uniform as he shifted from foot to foot.

She caught Meli's arm, pulling her beneath the gallery's awning. "The poor man looks like he's been there for hours." Her gaze flicked between the tea rooms and the young constable as a plan formed. "He must be desperate for a break by now?"

A smile tugged at Meli's lips. "And I suppose you'd like me to suggest one?"

"Purely in the public interest, of course. It wouldn't do to have a member of the constabulary passing out from heatstroke now, would it?"

The constable snapped to attention as Meli approached, one hand rising to adjust his helmet while perspiration trickled down his temple. "I'm sorry, miss, but no one's allowed up these stairs."

"I wouldn't dream of it. But I couldn't help noticing that you've been standing here since first thing and you look like you could do with a cooling drink." Meli's voice held just the right note of sympathy.

"Thank you for your concern, miss, but I've got my orders." The constable squared his shoulders, tugging at his damp collar.

"But it's such a hot day, and the tea rooms are just across the way there. I'm sure the Chief Inspector wouldn't mind your taking a few minutes out of the sun to cool down."

The constable's gaze drifted toward the Palace Pier Tea Rooms, his Adam's apple bobbing as sweat trickled past his collar.

"The door's locked, isn't it?" She glanced at the heavy brass handle. "And you could just as easily keep an eye on the stairs perfectly well from one of the window tables." Meli tilted her head, gazing up at him from beneath her dark lashes. "A nice cool glass of ginger beer would set you up a treat for the rest of your shift."

Elizabeth watched from behind a potted palm as the constable shifted his weight, his gaze darting between Meli's encouraging smile and the promise of shade in the tea rooms opposite.

"I don't know, miss..." The constable tugged at his collar again. "If the Chief Inspector found out I'd left my post, he'd have my guts for garters."

"Just ten minutes," Meli coaxed. "He won't even know you were gone."

The moment they entered the tea rooms, Elizabeth darted up the stairs, avoiding the second step. Two hairpins from her bag made quick work of the lock, and she eased the door open just enough to slip inside.

Daylight flooded through the sash windows at either end of the studio as Elizabeth eased the door shut, transforming Vale's studio from the shadowed space she'd explored the previous night.

Glass bottles crowded Vale's work table, each surface a canvas of dried paint drips and smudged fingerprints. Elizabeth lifted the nearest one to her nose, her head snapping back as paint thinner seared her nostrils and made her eyes water. She set it down and sniffed the contents of a second bottle – this one held only the sharp, clean traces of turpentine. Among the artist's supplies, a dark green bottle caught her eye – its shape unmistakably that of a whisky bottle. Elizabeth uncorked it and breathed in the familiar spirits, but beneath the whisky fumes, an earthy undertone similar to the one she'd smelt last night. Valerian root.

Why would anyone want to ruin the taste of whisky with such a pungent sedative?

Elizabeth surveyed the studio. Empty jam jars lay on their sides, paint brushes and discarded paint tubes scattered across the floor, canvases askew. The disarray nagged at her – was this simply Vale's bohemian existence, or had someone been rifling through his things?

Her gaze caught on something protruding from behind a stack of canvases; a thin mattress, rolled and wedged against the wall. If Vale was living here, he clearly didn't want Vivi to know.

But why stay in a studio without even the basic amenities when he'd recently sold his painting, *Tuscan Spring*, for fifty guineas?

Elizabeth sifted through the stack of paintings leaning against the wall. Most were unfinished landscapes, a few still-life paintings, until her hand stilled on a canvas that shared the unmistakable style of Rosalind's portrait. Another from the *Nymphaeum* series, though this one struck a different tone entirely. The model reclined on silk drapes that preserved her modesty, her face turned away from the viewer.

Something in the curve of her neck and the glossy dark locks reminded Elizabeth of Essie, but the angle made it impossible to be certain. Elizabeth studied the canvas again. If this was Essie's portrait, why had she been so terrified of anyone seeing it?

A leather portfolio lay half-hidden beneath loose sketches. Elizabeth drew it out, careful not to disturb the surrounding papers. Inside, charcoal drawings captured a scene at one of Soho's bohemian coffee houses – the cramped tables and smoke-stained walls suggesting the kind of establishment where artists and writers gathered.

One sketch drew her eye – a woman throwing her head back in laughter, her vitality radiating from the page even in those few swift strokes. Next to her, Vivi's younger self shared in the merriment, their joy infectious even through the charcoal lines. Rosalind's words echoed in Elizabeth's mind … *According to Vale, you two were something of an item, back in your Gaiety Girl days.*

A figure burst from behind a privacy screen, shouldering past Elizabeth with such force she stumbled backwards. By the time she regained her balance, the intruder was already half-way through the window.

She rushed after him, reaching it just in time to see a man scrambling across the neighbouring rooftops, before lowering himself down onto the pier and disappearing into the crowd.

Elizabeth steadied herself against the window frame. Even in that brief glimpse, she'd caught the distinctive details – the frayed tweed jacket, those paint-spattered boots. The same outfit worn by the man who'd unsettled Vivi in the gallery last night.

The Brighton Queen's whistle echoed across the pier as Elizabeth darted from the window where the intruder had vanished to the opposite one overlooking the tearooms. Through the salt-hazed glass, she watched Meli and the constable push back their chairs, her cousin's face angled towards the studio. *Time to leave*. Elizabeth returned the portfolio among Vale's sketches and eased open the door to check the coast was clear.

She crept down the stairs, keeping close to the wall. Meli gestured towards the steamer as it glided past the pier, keeping the constable's attention firmly in the opposite direction. In her haste, Elizabeth forgot about the second step, catching her heel on the broken tread. She grabbed the wooden handrail to steady herself, biting back a gasp as rough wood bit into her palm.

The constable turned, his eyes widening as he spotted her. "Here, miss!" He made to give chase. "Stop right there!"

A procession of WI ladies blocked his path, their straw hats bobbing in unison as they followed their leader's raised umbrella towards the Palace Pier Tea Rooms. "This way, ladies, no dawdling."

Elizabeth ducked into the amusement arcade, weaving between holidaymakers at the slot machines, before slipping out the opposite entrance and melting into the crowd.

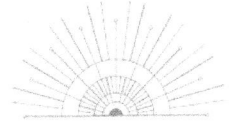

Chapter Ten

ELIZABETH EASED THE VAUXHALL around a delivery van, narrowly avoiding a baker's boy, his arms piled high with fresh loaves still warm from the ovens. She winced as she adjusted her grip on the steering wheel, the wooden splinter lodged in her palm a painful reminder of her hasty escape from Vale's studio.

Along Kings Road, the Metropole's entrance hummed with morning arrivals – porters hefting leather trunks while well-dressed guests navigated the bustle, their morning chatter rising above the clink of brass luggage trolleys against the stone steps.

"The studio was in complete disarray; I can't tell if that was the intruder's work or just Vale's habits. The rolled-up mattress suggested he was living there, which seems strange given Sir Geoffrey Ward paid fifty guineas for one of his paintings not three months back."

Meli twisted in her seat, her dark curls lifting in the breeze. "Perhaps he's spent it?"

"All of it?" Elizabeth considered her cousin's words. "It's possible, I suppose, but there's nothing to show for such a sum – no fine clothes, no luxuries, nothing of any real value at all."

"Do you think Vivi knew he was living there?"

"I wouldn't have thought so." Elizabeth turned right off Kings Road, onto Adelaide Crescent. "Not the way his mattress was hidden away."

The Vauxhall's wheels crunched against gravel as she guided the motorcar through the iron side gate. Her fingers shifted against the steering wheel, adjusting their grip to avoid the tender spot in her palm.

"Who do you think the intruder was?"

"An artist, I'd say, from the paint splats on his clothes." Elizabeth eased off the accelerator as they approached the coach house. "Whoever he is, he certainly had an unsettling effect on Vivi last night at the exhibition."

"Could he be the one we heard her arguing with?"

"Possibly." Elizabeth shrugged. "But with Vale using the studio as well, it could just as easily have been him."

Elizabeth brought the car to a halt inside the coach house, pain shooting through her palm as she released the steering wheel.

"That needs attention." Meli nodded towards Elizabeth's hand as they crossed the scullery threshold.

Meli searched through the kitchen cupboards one by one until she found a metal tin of medical supplies. At the scullery table, she laid out tweezers, cotton wool, and a small bottle of iodine.

"Blasted step." Elizabeth muttered, extending her palm.

"You're fortunate a splinter is all you got." Meli steadied Elizabeth's hand.

The low timbre of a man's voice carried down the hall. "It sounds like Gigi has a visitor."

Meli steadied the tweezers, drawing the splinter free from Elizabeth's skin. The brief pinch of extraction gave way to the cool sting of iodine as Meli dabbed the cotton wool against the wound.

"Do you want a plaster?"

"No, indeed." Elizabeth shook her head. "It's only a little pinprick."

"Someone's been in the wars, I see." Mrs Bramley bustled into the kitchen, heading straight for the kettle. "Will you be joining Miss Essie and Mr Pembroke in the sitting-room? I'm just preparing a fresh pot of tea."

Meli caught Elizabeth's eye at the mention of Pembroke's name.

"Tea would be lovely, Mrs Bramley." Elizabeth rose, Meli following suit as she reached for the tin of medical supplies.

"Oh, don't you go troubling yourself with that, Miss Meli." Mrs Bramley's hand fluttered in the air. "I'll see to it."

"If you're sure?"

"As sure as eggs is eggs." Mrs Bramley picked up the tin. "Now why don't you wait in the sitting-room? Tea will be ready in five minutes"

Meli touched Elizabeth's sleeve as they made their way along the hall to the sitting-room. "What do you think Pembroke is doing here?"

"I don't know, but we're about to find out." Elizabeth pitched her voice to carry as she entered first, Meli a step behind. "I've never seen anything–Oh, I'm terribly sorry, I didn't realise..."

Elizabeth paused at the sight of Pembroke and Essie on the sofa, his hands cradling hers.

Essie snatched her hands from Pembroke's grasp, a flush creeping across her face.

"I do apologise for interrupting. We can–"

"No." Pembroke shifted on the sofa. "Please stay. Your timing is perfect, actually. Essie and I … we owe you an explanation."

Elizabeth settled into one armchair, Meli taking the other.

"Essie and I met in Tuscany, at Gigi's parent's villa. I was there visiting Chaz before his posting to Nairobi."

"I didn't know you two were acquainted," Elizabeth said.

"Yes, we were at Eton and then Cambridge together."

Meli leaned forward in her chair. "Forgive my interruption, but who's Chaz?"

Elizabeth turned to her. "Charles, Gigi's older brother. He's a doctor with the Red Cross."

"When I returned to England," Pembroke continued. "Essie and I corresponded. At first it was just friendship, but over the months, our feelings changed, they became more romantic in nature. And when Essie returned to England with Gigi, well … we've been seeing each other ever since."

"But why all the secrecy?"

"It was Essie's choice." Pembroke glanced at Essie.

"Vale." She twisted her hands in her lap. "I didn't know Vale was in Brighton; the last I'd heard of him, he was in France." Essie's voice dropped. "But he saw us together, and threatened to expose me and my pa–the painting. And I couldn't risk him exposing me and ruining Laurie's campaign."

Elizabeth caught Essie's slip. *Had she been about to say something else*?

"Vale took advantage of Essie when she was struggling in Tuscany, convinced her to pose for that painting." Pembroke's voice tightened. "Then he hid behind her to blackmail me."

"I can see why you wouldn't want something like this being made public during your campaign."

"My campaign?" Pembroke shook his head. "You're mistaken, Lady Elizabeth. My only concern is for Essie." He took her hand. "We intend to marry, you see, but Essie has refused to set a date until this business with the police is settled."

"It's not just the campaign." Essie's shoulders dropped. "There's your father's health to consider."

His gaze flicked between Elizabeth and Meli. "My father's health has been precarious these last six months and Essie didn't want any hint of scandal to hinder his recovery." He paused. "That's why I arranged her bail, kept her name from the papers. The Chief Constable agreed to withhold it for a week while Walsh pursued other leads. But if they find no other suspects by then..."

"I'm sure Chief Inspector Walsh is working on new leads as we speak." Elizabeth tried to reassure them.

"Walsh? As far as he's concerned, the case is solved. He and Sir Lionel Grimwald and their set see crime in everything modern. Young people, liberal attitudes, anything that challenges their narrow view of the world. Walsh won't waste time looking elsewhere; you can be sure of that. Thankfully we don't have to rely on him now. Gigi tells me you've agreed to investigate Vale's murder. She says you're quite the detective."

"Please don't put too much store in what Gigi says, she has a habit of exaggerating my capabilities."

"You're too modest, Lady Elizabeth. I read all about the Reggie Black case in the newspapers."

"I couldn't have done it without Meli's help."

"Not to mention that business up at Mayfield Manor." Pembroke raised a brow.

How on earth did Pembroke know about the Mayfield Manor murder? It hadn't made the newspapers like Black's case had. It had been *dealt with* discretely at the highest level

"I'm curious, Mr Pembroke, how you knew about Mayfield Manor?"

"Oh, Ashcroft and I go back years."

Jonathan Ashcroft. A man who had a knack for turning up in the most unexpected places, who seemed to know everyone while remaining unknowable himself.

"My parents return from their overseas trip in five days, and I'd hoped to introduce Essie to them before all this happened. So, if there's anything you can do to find the real culprit before then, I–we'd be extremely grateful."

"I can't make any promises, but we'll do our best."

"That's all anyone can ask. And if I can be of help in any way, you only need ask." He rose. "Forgive me for dashing off, but I have a meeting with the Ladies' Relief Society in half an hour."

Essie stood. "I'll see you out."

Meli waited until the footsteps faded. "Why didn't you mention that we'd been to Vale's studio this morning? Or the intruder?"

Elizabeth's thoughts returned to the night of the murder, to the moment she'd spotted Pembroke slipping back into the gallery. Where had he been? She couldn't be sure how long he'd been absent, but with Vale's studio just upstairs, there would have been time enough for a young man like Pembroke to slip upstairs, murder Vale, and return to the gallery within minutes.

"You don't think Pembroke could have murdered Vale, do you?"

"I'm not sure yet, but his revelations about his relationship with Essie and his father's ill health mean that he had motive enough to want Vale silenced."

"But if he was the murderer, would he really leave Essie, the woman he claims to love, to face the gallows?"

Elizabeth's mind circled back to Essie herself. She had been found with the murder weapon in her hand, standing over the victim's dead body.

Yet Elizabeth struggled to reconcile the idea that Essie was capable of such violence. But she still couldn't shake the feeling Essie wasn't being entirely honest with them.

A thought struck her, dark and troubling.

Was it possible they were in it together?

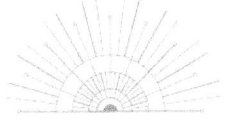

Chapter Eleven

THE MUSLIN CURTAINS BILLOWED in the morning breeze as Elizabeth cradled her teacup, her gaze drifting past the window to where Mr Bramley tended his roses in the garden beyond. Her breakfast long since forgotten as each piece of yesterday's puzzle refused to align – the rolled-up mattress hidden away in Vale's studio, the whisky laced with valerian, the mysterious intruder and, of course, the sketch of Vivi in her younger days she'd found tucked among the canvases.

Essie's overreaction to her *Nymphaeum* painting presented another conundrum.

Then there was Pembroke's confession about his and Essie's marriage plans. Was Vale's death a happy misfortune or a convenient solution to their dilemma?

"There's an article here about Rosalind and Stacey." Meli pushed aside her breakfast plate, her eyes widening. "In Mrs Drummond-Ward's *About Town* column of all places."

"Really?" Elizabeth set down her teacup.

"One simply couldn't miss the spectacle at The Lux last evening." Meli began reading aloud. *"Young Mr Stacey Grimwald, Judge Grimwald's only son, and the irrepressible Miss Rosalind Delacourt, engaged in what could scarcely be called polite conversation. Whether Sir Lionel will be amused to find his heir apparent so comfortably ensconced with Brighton's most notorious flirt is anyone's guess – particularly given the recent artistic revelations at the Palace Pier Exhibition Rooms."*

"Strange. It must be a misprint. It's Tommy Rosalind is in love with." Elizabeth's finger circled the rim of her teacup. "Haven't you seen the way she reacts whenever he speaks to another woman, especially poor Sylvia."

"No, no misprint. There's a photograph, look." Meli turned the page towards her cousin. "Taken by none other than Mr Jimmy Morton."

Elizabeth studied the photograph of the pair at their corner table at The Lux, Rosalind's face alight with laughter, while Stacey's hand rested near hers on the crisp white tablecloth.

"The Judge's son and Brighton's most notorious flirt." Meli spread the newspaper across the breakfast table. "I'm sure Sir Lionel will have something to say about this."

"I'm sure he will." Elizabeth's eyes followed Mr Bramley as he turned his attention to the sweet peas. "I've been thinking. Perhaps we should pay Vivi a visit, see if she can shed some light on the identity of the intruder. Gigi mentioned she has another gallery on Western Road, which is practically on our doorstep."

"Do you think she knows him?"

"His presence certainly seemed to unsettle her at the exhibition."

Meli pushed away from the table, rising. "Just give me a few minutes to fetch my bag."

Elizabeth collected her hat and gloves from the hall table, securing her cloche with a mother-of-pearl-tipped hatpin in the mirror.

"Ready?" She caught Meli's reflection as she descended the stairs.

"As I'll ever be."

The walk from Adelaide Crescent took them past the neat front gardens where hollyhocks reached skyward against white-painted walls. At the corner, a young housemaid worked at the brass door fittings, her apron pockets bulging with polishing cloths.

They turned into Western Road's morning bustle. Outside Palmer's Bakery, the scent of fresh bread mingled with the crisp sweetness of dahlias from Mr Collins' flower cart. His small son darted between the zinc buckets, water splashing his boots as he called out prices in a voice too big for his years. At Gorringe's corner, a cluster of ladies in summer frocks paused their discussion of window displays to let the baker's boy pass, his cart wheels clanking against the cobbles as he threaded his way through the growing crowd.

V. Marchant Fine Art gleamed in gold lettering between Madame Fournier's Millinery and Perkins' Tea Room.

"This must be it." Meli paused outside the narrow doorway.

The door burst outward. Sir Lionel Grimwald barged between them, his face mottled with rage. He paused, dabbing his forehead with a handkerchief; white gauze stark against his sallow skin where it wrapped his right hand.

"Sir Lionel, is everything all right–"

He thrust past them, cutting off Elizabeth's words as he vanished into the morning crowd.

"How rude." Meli drew herself up to her full height, chin tilted, toffee-coloured eyes flashing.

"Indeed." Elizabeth raised an eyebrow. "Perhaps Vivi can shed some light on the reason he was in such a foul mood."

She pushed open the gallery door, the brass bell signalling their arrival. Vivi turned from a display of watercolours as they entered, her smile brittle.

"Lady Elizabeth and Miss Diomaros." Her voice pitched higher than usual as she moved between an elegant bronze and a marble plinth bearing a small sculpture. "What a lovely surprise."

"I didn't realise you had another gallery here on Western Road." Elizabeth's gaze swept past gilt-framed landscapes to a collection of ceramics. "We're almost neighbours, well, whilst we're staying at Adelaide Crescent, that is."

"Ten years this autumn."

"What about the pier gallery?"

"That's seasonal, aimed at the summer tourists. Or at least it was before…"

"Forgive my impertinence, and I wouldn't want to pry, but we had an encounter with Sir Lionel Grimwald on our way in. He seemed rather preoccupied."

"He disapproves of young Stacey's career choices and came here to insist I stop encouraging him. Sir Lionel believes his son should follow in his footsteps."

"It's so often the way with fathers, isn't it? Wanting their sons to continue the family legacy. How fortunate we are as daughters to have no greater expectations thrust upon us than to be someone's wife and mother."

"Very true, Lady Elizabeth, though some legacies are born, while others are made." She busied herself straightening a frame. "Tell me, how is Miss Baker bearing up?"

"As well as can be expected under the circumstances."

"Have they charged her?"

"Not as far as I'm aware."

"What about you? Have you given your statement to the police yet?"

"I haven't, but I'm sure it's only a matter of time before they contact me. Such a dreadful business, wasn't it?" Elizabeth tilted her head as she met Vivi's gaze. "And it must be difficult for you. I understand you knew him well?"

"We moved in the same circles many moons ago, though I hadn't seen him for years." Vivi's hand fluttered through the air, dismissing the weight of their connection. "That's why I was so surprised when he turned up at the gallery some months back, asking me to represent him. I was hesitant, of course, knowing him as I did, but he claimed he'd given up drinking and was a changed man." Her fingers fidgeted with her pearls. "And the work … well, it was better than ever."

"So you agreed?"

"I'd have been a fool not to."

"I'd heard Vale's career had gone through something of a renaissance after Sir Geoffrey Ward bought one of his paintings for fifty guineas."

"Yes, well … there's been a minor hiccup there."

"Hiccup?"

"It's nothing." Vivi shifted her attention to a small figurine, adjusting it a fraction to the right. "Just a few i's need dotting, you know how these things are."

"Would you mind if I had a look around?" Meli asked. "You have some lovely pieces."

"Be my guest."

"Was Vale planning to settle in Brighton, do you know?" Elizabeth steered the conversation back to Vale. "I understand from my cousin that he spent a lot of time in Italy."

"Who knows with Vale." Vivi shrugged. "He said he was waiting for some windfall, claimed it would set him up for life."

"Did he mention what this windfall might be?"

"I assumed it was a sale. He'd been talking about having a buyer for the *Nymphaeum* series. Perhaps that was it."

"Ah, yes." Elizabeth kept her tone light. "Were you familiar with it?"

"Somewhat. He used to say it was his passion project, something about the dichotomy of woman. It began with a portrait of a friend of mine, Alice Ellis. We were Gaiety Girls together back then." A smile touched her lips. "Alice used to model for him."

"What about you?"

"Oh no." Vivi's laugh held a brittle edge. "Alice was the beauty. Had men falling over themselves for her attention. But she only had eyes for Vale ... no matter how badly he treated her."

"Are you still in touch with Alice?"

"No." Vivi's gaze drifted to the window. "She married, and her husband didn't approve of her old friends. Last I heard, she'd left him and gone to America." Her voice softened. "Leaving young Stacey behind."

Elizabeth's breath caught. Sir Lionel Grimwald had been married to a Gaiety Girl?

"It seems strange for a mother to leave without her child, though."

"I thought so too, at first. Stacey was such a sweet boy, and Alice doted on him." A shadow crossed Vivi's face. "But Sir Lionel made her life so miserable, I think she felt she had no choice but to leave. And she'd never have won if she'd tried to fight for custody in the courts; not with his connections and money. I always believed she'd come back for Stacey, but…" She trailed off with a small shrug.

"And you've never heard from her since? Not in all these years?"

"No … I just assumed she'd made a new life for herself in America." Vivi's gaze returned to the window. "Perhaps keeping in touch would have been too painful, a reminder of the child she left behind."

Elizabeth let the silence linger before changing the subject. "Do you remember the man you spoke to at the exhibition, just before Vale's unveiling of Rosalind's portrait? His face looked familiar, but I can't place him."

"I'm afraid you'll have to be more specific, Lady Elizabeth. I spoke to a lot of men that night."

"Tall fellow, tweed jacket, long brown hair?"

"No one comes to mind. He was likely an artist hawking his portfolio; it happens all the time."

"Perfectly understandable. I'm sure any artist worth their salt would give their eye-teeth for wall space here, wouldn't you agree, Meli?"

"Indeed, I would. I've just been admiring the exquisite glass lamps over there."

"They are rather special, aren't they? The artist's a young Austrian chap who settled here after the war."

The brass bell above the door chimed as a well-dressed couple entered.

"We won't keep you any longer." Elizabeth inclined her head towards the newcomers.

"Lady Elizabeth–" Vivi glanced at the couple, then lowered her voice. "Before you go, has there been any word on the post-mortem? Or the coroner's inquest date?"

"Not that I'm aware of. Are you concerned about being called?"

"I ... yes, a little, if I'm honest."

"I can assure you there's nothing to worry about." Elizabeth placed a hand on Vivi's arm. "All you have to do is tell the truth."

"Yes … yes, I'm sure you're right. I'm sure I'm just overthinking the whole thing."

The well-dressed couple hovered near a seascape, the gentleman clearing his throat.

"We should let you attend to your business." Elizabeth turned towards the door. "It was lovely to see you again, Vivi."

The brass bell chimed as they exited the gallery.

"Well, that was enlightening."

"You can say that again." Meli matched her pace to Elizabeth's as they made their way along Western Road. "I can't believe the very proper Judge Grimwald was married to a Gaiety Girl, or that she was involved with Vale."

"Nor can I."

"Though I'm not sure whose behaviour was more peculiar, Sir Lionel's or Vivi's."

"Yes, she's certainly given us plenty to think about. The man she professed not to know visibly rattled her that night, so I suspect she's lying."

"What about Vale's domestic arrangements? Do you think she knows he was living there?"

"Hard to tell. If she did, she didn't let on." They paused at the kerb as a motorcar rattled past. "But I must confess Vale's living arrangements puzzle me."

"How so?" Meli's brow creased.

"My initial thoughts were why was a man who'd sold a painting for such a sum be living like a vagrant, but there was something Vivi said about there being a hiccup in the sale with Sir Geoffrey Ward that makes me wonder whether he'd received any of that money. And then there's the question of this mysterious windfall that he was waiting on, that would set him up for life."

"What if this windfall wasn't from the sale of his paintings? What if it was the payment he was expecting from Essie and Pembroke?"

"Blackmail money? It would explain his claim about being set up for life. After all, blackmailers rarely settle for a single payment."

Meli sidestepped a woman with a pram. "That would explain Vale's confidence about his future income."

"Something else I found odd was Vivi's concern about the post-mortem."

"Now that you mention it, she seemed quite anxious about it."

"Vivi strikes me as someone who's faced far worse than a coroner's inquest in her time." Elizabeth slowed her pace as they turned onto Adelaide Crescent. "I need to speak with Pembroke to see if he can obtain a copy of Vale's post-mortem report."

"Why? Do you think she–"

"Well, we know someone was adding valerian to Vale's whisky. If it was Vivi, she had both means and opportunity." Elizabeth paused at their front gate.

"The question is, why?"

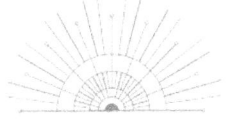

Chapter Twelve

MELI REACHED FOR THE marmalade, Mr Bramley's tuneless whistle drifting through the open windows as he polished Gigi's motorcar. Straightening, he ran the back of his hand across his brow as the June sun promised another scorching day.

"Are you sure you don't mind?" Gigi glanced at the clock on the mantelpiece. "I feel dreadful abandoning you like this, especially after last night, but I'd quite forgotten about the tennis tournament Rosalind signed us up for."

"Of course, we don't mind." Elizabeth reached for the teapot and refilled her cup.

"But I feel terrible. You came here for a holiday only to find yourself in the middle of a murder enquiry, not to mention last night's dinner with Cousin Eugenia."

"She's not so bad, really. And it wasn't a complete loss."

Elizabeth recalled how the evening's dinner conversation had yielded unexpected intelligence. A few discrete inquiries had revealed the scandal Sir Lionel's marriage to *that showgirl* had caused among Brighton's respectable families. Stacey's arrival less than eight months after the wedding had only added fuel to the fire, with Cousin Eugenia lamenting how *that girl* had made a complete fool of him. Sir Lionel had been besotted, according to their elderly cousin, and it had been a blessing for everyone, particularly the boy, when Alice had left for America.

"I still can't quite believe it." Gigi adjusted the pleated hem of her tennis whites. "Stacey's mother, a Gaiety Girl. Not that there's anything wrong with that, of course, but Sir Lionel…" She shook her head.

Lily cleared her throat as she entered the morning-room. "Excuse me, miss, but there's a telephone call for you. It's Miss Delacourt."

"Thank you, Lily." Gigi set her napkin beside her plate and rose.

Elizabeth waited until Gigi's footsteps faded. "I've been thinking about Gigi and her friendship with Essie. There's just something about Essie's story…" Elizabeth's voice dropped. "I can't shake the feeling she's still hiding something."

"And you're worried that if we tell Gigi, she could then pass it on to Essie?"

"Exactly." Elizabeth pushed her cup aside. "I think perhaps we should be more selective about what we tell her."

"I agree." Meli reached for the last triangle of toast. "Did Pembroke confirm he'd be able to secure a copy of the postmortem?"

"He said he'd try. Though given how protective the Chief Inspector is being about the entire investigation…" Elizabeth's words trailed into silence as Gigi's footsteps grew louder.

Gigi returned to the morning-room, her earlier enthusiasm gone. "Well, that's it for the tennis tournament. We might as well cancel the whole thing. Rosalind's had an accident."

"What happened?" Meli set down the butter knife. "Is she all right?"

"Just a sprained wrist, nothing serious." Gigi waved away their concern. "She claims someone pushed her on the stairs last night at the theatre." She dropped back down onto her chair with a sigh. "Though knowing Rosalind, she probably had one too many glasses of champagne and missed her footing. She loves to turn everything into a drama."

"But cancelling the tournament seems a bit extreme," Elizabeth said.

"There were only a handful of us left in, and now with Rosalind's wrist and Essie withdrawing to avoid unwanted attention…" Gigi shook her head. "Poor Stacey … it's far too late to find another partner now."

"Unless…" Elizabeth glanced at Meli. "You could take Rosalind's place?"

"You play tennis?" Gigi straightened in her chair.

"A little. Though I haven't picked up a racquet since we returned from France."

"It would give you a chance to speak to Stacey." Elizabeth met Meli's gaze.

"That's settled then." Gigi pushed back her chair. "I've got a spare set of tennis whites that should fit you. Shall we?"

Meli followed Gigi from the breakfast room, their excited chatter fading as they climbed the stairs.

Elizabeth carried her morning papers and a fresh cup of tea to the sitting-room, choosing the window seat overlooking the communal gardens.

Elizabeth had barely opened the newspaper when Maudie appeared in the doorway, feather duster in hand.

"Oh, I beg your pardon, my lady. I can come back–"

"That's quite all right, Maudie. Please don't let me stop you."

A-HOO-ga!

The feather duster stilled mid-swipe as Maudie stretched up on tiptoe, her bottom lip caught between her teeth while she craned for a better view of the road.

She inched sideways along the cabinet, the feather duster sweeping aimless circles closer and closer to the crystal vase of roses.

CRASH!

Maudie leapt back, her hand flying to her mouth as the crystal vase shattered against the floor. "Oh, my lady, I'm so sorry … I didn't mean…"

"Here, let me help–"

"No, Miss, you mustn't … Mrs Bramley's going to have my guts for garters … I'll most likely get the sack."

"What on earth?" Mrs Bramley bustled into the sitting-room, wiping her hands on her apron. "Lady Elizabeth, you shouldn't be down there on your hands and knees; let Maudie see to it."

A-HOO-ga!

Beyond the window, Tommy leaned against the bonnet of his Bentley, tossing a tennis ball up in the air and catching it, his tennis whites brilliant against the dark green paintwork.

Mrs Bramley's eyes darted to the window, her lips thinning. "If you'd paid more attention to your work and less to what's going on outside…" She shook her head. "Go fetch some cloths from the kitchen to mop up that water."

Maudie shuffled past Mrs Bramley, her chin tucked to her chest.

"That girl will be the death of me." The words escaped with a huff as Mrs Bramley tugged her apron straight.

Elizabeth straightened, handing Mrs Bramley several of the larger pieces of crystal. "It was my fault; I distracted her."

A-HOO-ga!

"That racket will have everyone in Preston Street Cemetery rattling in their coffins." Mrs Bramley placed the crystal fragments on the side table. "In my day, young men knew the proper way to call on a young lady."

Maudie slipped back into the room, cloths bundled in her arms, her attention drifting past Mrs Bramley to the window.

"Heaven preserve us." Mrs Bramley plucked the cloths from Maudie's arms. "Make yourself useful and go help Lily with the laundry."

"Oh, honestly." Gigi and Meli stepped into the sitting-room, tennis racquets in hand. "Tommy could learn a thing or two from our Mediterranean cousins."

"*Piano, piano,*" Meli said.

"*Precisamente.*"

"Are you sure you won't join us?" Meli asked.

"Thank you, but I think I'll go for a walk to clear my head instead."

"Take a drive down the front. I'm sure the sea air will blow away the cobwebs."

A-HOO-ga!

"I think we'd better go before Mrs B has a coronary. Wish us luck."

"Good luck."

Elizabeth rested her head against the wooden window recess as she watched Tommy's Bentley pull away from Adelaide Crescent.

The investigation had stalled at every turn: Vivi denied knowing the intruder, and Sir Lionel was hardly likely to discuss his past marriage with someone who had no authority to ask.

Even her suspicions about Pembroke lacked any real substance.

No matter how many times she tried to unravel all the loose ends, everything always circled back to Essie as the most credible suspect.

Perhaps Gigi was right.

A drive along the seafront might help lift the fog clouding her brain.

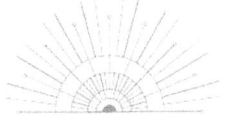

Chapter Thirteen

Elizabeth steered Gigi's carmine Vauxhall through the morning traffic along Kings Road. A newspaper boy darted between motorcars and delivery wagons, his cry of "Brighton Gazette. Murderer still at large. Read all about it." rising above the rumble of engines and clip of hooves. A steam tram rattled past, scattering pigeons skyward, their sudden flight startling a well-dressed woman into a shriek.

Elizabeth's grip tightened on the steering wheel. No matter how she looked at it, all logical roads led to the same conclusion – Essie was the killer. Yet, her instincts argued otherwise.

She slowed the motorcar, watching for a parking space along the promenade. A Morris Cowley pulled away, leaving a gap between an

Austin 12 and a baker's van. Elizabeth guided the Vauxhall into the space and cut the engine.

She reached into her handbag for her silver compact, angling it to check the tilt of her summer hat against the sun. With a decisive snap, she returned the compact to her bag before alighting from the Vauxhall.

The promenade stretched ahead, Brighton's summer season in full swing. Holidaymakers reclined in striped deck chairs beneath parasols, while children raced around the ornamental gardens in pursuit of wheeling gulls. A Punch and Judy show drew peals of laughter from a gathering of youngsters, their nursemaids deep in conversation nearby.

Elizabeth threaded her way between zinc buckets brimming with lupins and sweet peas as the flower seller arranged her morning display. A barrel organ's melody mingled with the clink of pennies dropping into a monkey's red cap, its tiny paw extended to passing children.

A cluster of onlookers surrounded the promenade artists near the bandstand. Elizabeth drew closer, intrigued by the array of easels and sketch pads propped against the seafront railings.

Further along, a man bent over his sketchbook, the charcoal moving swiftly across the paper as he sketched caricatures for waiting couples. His long brown hair fell forward as he worked, veiling his features. When he lifted his head, Elizabeth recognised him instantly – the intruder from Vale's studio.

Their eyes met, recognition turning to panic. The charcoal dropped from his fingers as he bolted upright, his folding stool clattering against the ground.

"Wait–" The word died in Elizabeth's throat as he vaulted the promenade railings. A woman in a yellow hat shrieked, her parasol tumbling as holidaymakers scattered. He hit the shingle hard, stones spraying as he found his balance and raced along the beach towards Palace Pier.

Elizabeth turned back to the artist's pitch where his belongings lay strewn about – a worn leather satchel, the overturned stool, scattered sketches, an upturned tin of charcoal sticks.

She gathered the scattered sketches, noticing each bore the same bold signature in thick charcoal strokes: *Fenn*.

"Excuse me," Elizabeth called to one of the artists. "Do you know Fenn?"

"I know him, yes." The woman glanced up from her painting, brush poised mid-stroke. "But he keeps to himself ... fancies himself a cut above the rest of us."

"Do you know where I might find him?"

"Lives somewhere off Middle Street, I believe."

Elizabeth thanked her and gathered the last of Fenn's belongings into his satchel before heading back towards Kings Road to get her bearings.

Middle Street branched off the main road between a tobacconist's and a small hotel advertising sea views and continental breakfast. The street sloped upward, its modest boarding houses and converted flats catering to Brighton's year-round residents rather than its summer visitors.

Elizabeth paused outside a greengrocer's where a woman in a flour-dusted apron arranged potatoes in wooden crates. "Excuse me, I'm looking for someone called Fenn – he's an artist. I believe he lives somewhere on this street?"

The woman straightened, wiping her hands on her apron. "Fenn? Number thirty-seven, second floor." She gestured up the street. "Keeps odd hours, that one."

Number thirty-seven stood halfway along the street, a three-storey building with peeling paint around its windows and a front door that had seen better days, propped open by a wooden wedge.

"Hello?" Elizabeth called into the hallway, her voice echoing against bare walls as she adjusted her grip on Fenn's stool. "Hello?"

Elizabeth climbed to the second landing, past worn carpet runners pinned by tarnished brass rods. At the top, she tried the right-hand door without success, then crossed to the opposite side. From within came a shuffle of movement, followed by the slow rasp of a bolt. The door opened a crack, revealing Fenn's face, pink with exertion.

His eyes widened. The door slammed, but Elizabeth's foot was already in the gap.

"Mr Fenn, I only want to talk."

"I've got nothing to say … and it's Fenn."

"I'm sorry?"

"Just Fenn, no Mr."

"Of course, forgive me." Elizabeth slipped his leather satchel through the gap. "I have your portfolio and charcoals."

Fenn snatched them with a grunt.

"Although I'm afraid the space isn't wide enough to pass your stool through."

The silence stretched as he weighed his options.

"Who are you?" Fenn's grip on the door loosened.

"My name is Elizabeth."

"What do you want? Why are you here?"

"As I said, Mr–Fenn. I only want to talk."

Fenn retreated, opening the door wide enough for Elizabeth to enter.

Inside, canvases leaned against every available wall space. An easel dominated the small sitting-room, positioned to catch the light from the large sash window overlooking Middle Street.

A low table served as both palette and workspace, its surface a landscape of dried paint and stained rags. Brushes stood in jam jars filled with murky liquid, while tubes of paint – some squeezed flat, others barely touched – clustered around a chipped ceramic plate.

Despite the creative chaos, the finished canvases showed real skill – seascapes that captured Brighton's changing moods, portraits that revealed character in a few deft strokes. This was no amateur's hobby, but the serious workspace of an exceptional artist.

Fenn closed the door behind her, his back pressed against it. "What do you want?"

"As I said, I just want to talk. I'm ... a journalist writing a tribute piece about Jasper Vale." The lie caught in her throat. "His recent death has sparked renewed interest in his work, and I'm trying to understand his place in Brighton's artistic community."

He pushed away from the door, running a hand through his unkempt hair. 'That's rich.

What kind of tribute are you planning ... *In Memory of Jasper Vale – Thief*?"

Thief?

"Did you know him well?"

"Well enough to know he couldn't be trusted ... with anything."

"These landscapes are quite remarkable." Elizabeth moved closer to a collection of paintings stacked against one of the walls, her interest piqued by a canvas depicting stone bridges, riverbanks and quaint Breton cottages with their slate rooves. "Brittany, unless I'm very much mistaken?"

"Spare me the flannel. Elizabeth, was it? If it's a sycophantic piece you're after – all *Vale* was the greatest artist who ever lived – then I'm afraid you'll be sorely disappointed."

Elizabeth turned from the painting, holding his gaze. "Then please tell me the truth about Jasper Vale."

"You want the truth?" Fenn thrust his hands deep into his pockets, his shoulders rigid. "He was a parasite who fed off other people's talent after squandering his own."

"How long had you known him?"

"Fifteen or so years." Fenn shrugged. "I was fresh from art school when Vale took me under his wing. God, I thought he was brilliant back then … the great Jasper Vale deigning to notice my work. I was convinced he'd be my gateway to artistic glory." Fenn's mouth twisted. "Instead, he'd tear my work to shreds, claiming I'd never amount to anything … and whenever I stood up to him, he told me he was doing it for my own good and that I'd thank him later."

"What changed?"

"People started noticing me. My work was selling, galleries were interested … and I wasn't his eager student anymore. I was competition. That's when I saw Vale for what he really was … a man whose talent had dried up, who couldn't bear to watch anyone else succeed."

"Last year I was offered a six-month residency at the *Accademia Pietro Vannucci* in Perugia. It was an opportunity of a lifetime. But I needed someone to look after my studio here in Brighton. Vale offered, and I was desperate." Fenn's laughter held no humour, only bitterness. "He said it was the least he could do for an old friend."

"When I arrived back, three of my best paintings were gone. Vale claimed there'd been a break-in and shrugged it off. Then, two months ago, I opened The Studio, and there was one of my paintings, featured in an article about Sir Geoffrey Ward's private collection. *A fine example of Jasper Vale's recent renaissance*, they called it. *Tuscan Spring* … except it wasn't Tuscany at all. Any fool could see the cathedral in the painting was Orvieto, in Umbria, but Vale didn't even know enough to realise Siena Cathedral has three spires, while Orvieto has none."

Is that what Vivi had been referring to when she'd mentioned a hiccup in the sale of Vale's painting to Sir Geoffrey Ward?

"Did you confront Vale about it?"

"Of course I did, and Vivi Marchant too. But he just denied it, told me to prove it." Fenn's hands balled into fists at his sides. "And Vivi … she tried to make it all go away with money. Offered to compensate me, as she put it. But I didn't want her compensation. I wanted recognition for my work."

"Does Sir Geoffrey know?"

"Vivi told me she'd deal with it herself and needed time to speak with Vale and Sir Geoffrey." His voice hardened. "A week passed, then another. She stopped answering my messages and wouldn't see me at the gallery. That's why I went to the exhibition. I knew she couldn't miss her own opening night."

"Did you, er, speak with Vale at the exhibition?" Elizabeth tried to keep her voice light.

"What exactly are you suggesting, *Elizabeth*?" His eyes darkened as he took a half-step forward. "That I visited Vale after leaving the exhibition and killed him in a jealous rage over my painting?"

Elizabeth's throat tightened as her gaze darted about the room. They were two floors up, and her only escape was blocked by Fenn.

"You're asking an awful lot of questions for a journalist writing a tribute piece for an art magazine." He took another half-step forward, his hand hovering above a paint-encrusted palette knife on the easel tray. "Who did you say you worked for again?"

"I, er … I didn't." Elizabeth edged backwards, the weight of her situation settling like lead in the pit of her stomach.

She was alone in a stranger's flat … and not a single soul in Brighton knew where she was.

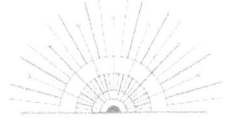

Chapter Fourteen

ELIZABETH'S HAND SLIPPED INSIDE her bag, finding the familiar weight nestled at the bottom. Her brother William's words echoed as her fingers brushed the metal barrel of her Browning Pocket Pistol – *trouble has a knack of finding you, Elizabeth, better to be safe than sorry*.

Fenn's hand moved past the palette knife, reaching for the packet of Gold Flake. "Cigarette?" He flicked it open, extending his hand towards Elizabeth.

The tension ebbed from her shoulders as her fingers loosened their grip on the Browning. "Thank you, but I don't smoke."

He shrugged, sliding a cigarette between his lips before striking a match. The flame flared as he cupped his hand around it, drawing the smoke deep into his lungs. "So who are you, really?" A grey curl escaped the corner of his mouth as he studied her.

"I'm not a journalist." Elizabeth withdrew her hand.

"That much is obvious." He crossed to the threadbare armchair and dropped into it, reaching for an empty jam jar among the brushes and turpentine bottles crowding the side table. "If you're not a journalist, what were you doing nosing around in Vale's studio?"

"My name is La-Elizabeth Hawthorne, and I'm trying to help a friend who's been implicated in Vale's murder."

"Then your friend is fortunate to have you, because God help them if they're counting on Walsh and his lot." He drew hard on his cigarette. "The Chief Inspector and his ilk have no time for anyone who doesn't fit their narrow little world. Art, modern ideas, people like ... us." He swept his hand wide, cigarette ash dusting the floorboards. "We're all guilty of something in his book."

"I'd like to ask you some questions, if you don't mind?"

"Ask away, I've got nothing to hide." Fenn ground out his cigarette on the ceramic saucer.

"What were you doing in Vale's studio the morning after his murder?"

"I could ask you the same question." His brow arched. "I was looking to see if he had the other paintings, the ones he'd claimed had been taken during the break-in when I was in Perugia."

"Did you find them?"

"I didn't have a chance to look before you showed up."

Elizabeth nodded, recalling his hasty escape across the rooftops. "Where were you around the time of Vale's murder?"

"I was working on the pier that evening, plenty of witnesses. During a lull, I went to the gallery to confront Vivi. She'd been avoiding me for weeks, but I knew she'd be there for Vale's exhibition."

"And then what?"

"She couldn't get rid of me quick enough, practically shoved me out the door."

"Mr-Fenn, I don't mean to be rude, but could you–"

"Hurry things along?" He tapped out another cigarette, striking a match against the box. "Two young women grabbed me the minute I stepped outside. They recognised me from the promenade the night before. They wanted their portraits done, even convinced some green constable to pose with them." The match flame wavered as he lit the cigarette. "Then a toff came tearing down the pier, dragging the constable off to some emergency."

Pembroke.

"I'd have paid good money to have seen the look on Walsh's face when he heard that, one of his own giving the likes of me an alibi." Fenn's mouth twisted into a smile. "Couldn't have planned it better myself."

Elizabeth couldn't fault his logic. A constable's testimony would carry weight in a court of law, no matter how much the Chief Inspector might wish otherwise.

"Thank you for your time, Fenn ... I won't keep you any longer." Elizabeth crossed to the door.

"Take my word for it, Miss Hawthorne." His words echoed after her down the stairs. "Whoever killed Vale did the world a favour."

Elizabeth squinted as she emerged onto Middle Street, the afternoon sun blinding after the gloom of Fenn's flat.

Fenn had reason enough to want revenge on Vale, but enough to kill him?

She'd seen Fenn's work, his skill evident in the canvases stacked against the walls. Yet while he'd spent his days sketching day-trippers on the pier for pennies, Vale had claimed both fame and fortune, passing off Fenn's painting as his own. Vale hadn't just stolen Fenn's work - he'd stolen his future.

Elizabeth turned onto Kings Road, weaving between the afternoon holidaymakers, while motorcars vied for parking space along the seafront.

Fenn's alibi was indeed watertight. A police constable and at least two other witnesses placed him on the pier around the time Vale was murdered.

Elizabeth made her way along the promenade to where the Vauxhall waited and slid in behind the wheel.

She let her head fall back against the seat. No matter where she looked or who she spoke to, the investigation always circled back to where it started – Essie.

A-HOO-ga!

A-HOO-ga!

Elizabeth lifted her head, catching sight of the impatient Morris Oxford driver gesturing towards her parking space. Turning on the engine, she slipped the motorcar into gear and pulled into the stream of traffic.

Her thoughts churned as she navigated the afternoon traffic back towards Adelaide Crescent. Her conversation with Fenn had yielded another dead end, yet his words lingered – *whoever killed Vale did the world a favour*. She turned into the sweeping curve of the crescent, guiding the motorcar through the iron gates and bringing it to a halt inside the coach house.

The stone path led her past Mrs Bramley's herbs to the scullery door. Inside, Essie stood at the counter measuring tea leaves into the pot.

"Don't tell Mrs B I'm using her kitchen." Essie glanced up, attempting a smile that didn't mask her exhaustion. "Tea?"

"Please." Elizabeth set her bag on the table, noting the dark circles under Essie's eyes, the way her hands trembled over the teapot.

"There was a telephone call while you were out, from the police station."

Elizabeth's stomach tightened. "Oh?"

"Chief Inspector Walsh will be here tomorrow morning at ten to speak to everyone." Tea leaves scattered across the counter as she caught the side of the teapot. "He was quite insistent that everyone make themselves available."

Essie reached for the cloth beside the sink.

"Let me help." Elizabeth stepped around her, setting out Mrs Bramley's best Wedgwood cups on a silver tray, while Essie poured freshly boiled water into the pot.

"Shall we take it into the sitting-room?" Elizabeth picked up the tray. "I'm sure we'll be more comfortable in there."

Elizabeth set down the tray on the coffee table before settling into one of the armchairs, while Essie took the sofa.

"I'm curious, what took you to Tuscany?" Elizabeth filled two cups, passing one to Essie. "Not many young women would be brave enough to travel so far alone."

"After my parents died, the church and a generous benefactor sponsored my training at Norland College. I'd always dreamed of seeing the world, so when the Contessa Visconti advertised for an English nanny for her daughters, it seemed like the perfect opportunity."

"It certainly sounds like it."

"Oh, it was. The Contessa treated me like family, and the girls…" A smile touched Essie's lips. "Lucia and Bianca were adorable. We'd have lessons in the mornings, then take walks in the afternoons collecting wildflowers."

Elizabeth studied Essie over the rim of her teacup. "If you were so happy there, why did you leave?"

Essie set down her tea. "There was a disagreement … about wages, and I was dismissed."

"Surely that could have been resolved?"

Essie's fingers twisted in her lap, her eyes darting between Elizabeth and the door.

"Essie." Elizabeth's voice softened. "I can't help you unless you tell me everything. No matter how painful the truth might be."

"But you don't understand. I..." Essie's voice caught. "If you knew what I'd done ... you'd think me such a wicked person."

If you knew what I'd done. Elizabeth's pulse thrummed in her ears. *Was Essie about to confess to Vale's murder?*

Elizabeth slid forward to the edge of her chair. "Whatever it is, Essie, you can tell me..."

"There was ... a man." Essie's shoulders curved inward, her breath escaping in ragged, uneven bursts. "A friend of the family, or so I believed."

"Go on."

"He began joining us on our afternoon walks. While I taught the girls about the birds and flowers, he'd weave tales of ancient ruins and hidden treasures. The children adored him. On my days off, we'd explore the Tuscan countryside together, winding through olive groves to discover remote villages and churches. He painted such pictures of our future together – the house we'd share, the garden we'd plant, the life we'd build. And I believed every word." Essie's hand drifted to her middle. "Now I see those drives for what they were. Not romantic adventures, but strategic choices – places where no one would recognise him."

Elizabeth noted the way Essie's palm rested against her abdomen. "Essie, forgive my indelicacy, but was there … a child?"

Essie nodded, unable to meet Elizabeth's gaze as she drew back into the corner of the sofa. "You must understand, I would never have … but he spoke of marriage with such certainty, that I … let my guard down." Her words faded into silence. "When I told him about … my condition, I thought he'd be happy, but that's when he told me he was already engaged to be married … to someone else."

"Did he end his engagement?"

Essie shook her head. "He was furious, accusing me of trying to trap him into marriage. Told me he'd never give up his fiancée's family fortune and position for a servant girl. Then I discovered his fiancée was the Contessa's cousin … and when she found out…" She drew in a shaky breath. "I was dismissed on the spot."

"Oh, Essie, I'm so sorry. How on earth did you manage?"

"I couldn't return to England. The thought of facing everyone…" Essie's voice dropped. "The vicar and his wife had been so proud when I earned my Norland certificate. After everything they'd done…" She stared into her teacup. "So, I remained in Tuscany and took whatever work came my way."

"And the child?"

Essie pressed her knuckles to her lips, tears pricking at her lash-line.

Elizabeth's heart ached as understanding dawned.

Essie had lost her child.

Elizabeth crossed to the sofa, taking Essie's hand in hers. "I am so very sorry, Essie." She kept her voice low, gentle. "Did Vale discover what happened in Tuscany?"

Essie nodded, her fingers tightening around Elizabeth's.

"And this is what he used against you?"

Another nod, smaller this time.

"We're back." Gigi's voice rang out as she and Meli made their way down the hallway.

"Please." Essie's grip tightened on Elizabeth's hand. "No one else knows. Not even Gigi."

"Your secret is safe with me." Elizabeth replied as Essie dabbed at her eyes with her fingertips. "I promise."

Elizabeth rose, positioning herself in front of Essie as Gigi and Meli entered, tennis racquets still in hand, their faces flushed with victory and sunshine.

"How did it go?" Elizabeth shifted her weight, maintaining her position between Essie and the doorway.

"Splendidly!" Meli's eyes sparkled as she collapsed into an armchair. "We won."

"You won?" Elizabeth raised an eyebrow. "Both of you? I thought it was mixed doubles."

"No, Meli and Stacey won," Gigi clarified, settling onto the arm of Meli's chair.

"Stacey was the real champion. Those crooked fingers of his didn't hinder his performance one bit."

"Crooked fingers?" Gigi's brow creased.

"His right hand – the fourth and fifth fingers curve inward." Meli flexed her own fingers in demonstration. "I'd assumed it was from some childhood accident, but apparently, they've been like that since birth. Haven't you ever noticed?"

"Can't say that I have, no. But it doesn't seem to affect his tennis game."

"Or his painting," Meli added.

"Speaking of which, we have wonderful news." Gigi's smile widened as her gaze darted between Elizabeth and Essie. "Stacey's invited us all for dinner tomorrow evening – for a double celebration."

"Double?" Essie peered around Elizabeth.

"Vivi sold one of his paintings yesterday." Gigi's smile widened. "Isn't it marvellous?"

Essie's shoulders dropped. "It is indeed, but I don't think I–"

"Ah, but that's exactly why Stacey suggested having it at his house." Gigi leaned forward. "And we needn't worry about Sir Lionel being there, spoiling everything. He's in London for a few days on court business, whatever that means." She brightened. "Please say you'll join us."

Elizabeth turned to Essie.

"What's wrong?" Gigi straightened, her gaze going from one to the other. "Has something happened?"

"There was a telephone call from the police station while you were out." Elizabeth watched Gigi's smile fade. "Chief Inspector Walsh will be here at ten tomorrow to take our statements."

"Really, he'd do far better spending his time finding the actual killer instead of badgering the innocent." Gigi rose. "I'm going to have a nice cool bath before dinner."

"And I think I'll rest for a while." Essie pushed herself up from the sofa. "Oh, Elizabeth." She paused in the doorway. "Mrs Bramley put a letter for you on the hall table. It arrived just after you left this morning."

Meli leaned forward in her chair. "Are you expecting something?"

"Not that I can recall." Elizabeth crossed to the hall table, returning with a crisp white envelope. She broke the seal as she sat, unfolding several typed pages. A post-mortem report. *Pembroke must have obtained a copy after all*.

Her eyes moved quickly across the page as she read.

Postmortem findings:

A severe laceration of the liver was present, with associated haemorrhage. Examination of the stomach revealed an abnormally large quantity of valerian, considerably above usual medicinal levels (noted).

Additional observation:

The fourth and fifth digits of the right hand were fixed in flexion and rigid at the joints, the fingers showing marked stiffness consistent with established rigidity.

Opinion:

Death resulted from haemorrhage due to hepatic laceration.

Elizabeth's brow creased as she re-read the pathologist's words.

O*f course*! "Kheset's Kiss."

"Kheset's Kiss?" Meli echoed.

"A hereditary condition passed through the male line, my father discovered it while excavating Pharaoh Sennefer's tomb. The mummy's right hand had a distinctive trait – the fourth and fifth digits curved inward. The hieroglyphs revealed Sennefer's male predecessors shared this same deformity."

"So, you think Vale had this Kheset's Kiss?"

"I believe so."

"But Stacey also has… Do you think Vale was Stacey's father?"

"I do, yes." Elizabeth held Meli's gaze. "But the question is… does Sir Lionel know?"

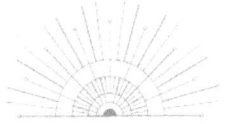

Chapter Fifteen

A COOLING BREATH OF air swept in through the bedroom window, carrying the briny tang of the English Channel while gulls shrieked overhead. From the street below came the muted clip of hooves and clink of bottles as the milk cart made its morning rounds along Adelaide Crescent.

"I don't know about you, but I barely slept a wink." Meli's voice drifted in and out as she rummaged through the wardrobe. "I couldn't stop thinking about Stacey and Vale ... and Kheset's Kiss. Do you really think Vale was Stacey's father?"

"Nothing's certain, but the pathologist's mention of the finger positions makes it likely." Elizabeth reached for her silver-backed brush on the bedside table, drawing it through her inky bob. "We know Vale was romantically involved with Stacey's mother before she married Sir Lionel. And don't forget Cousin Eugenia's comment about Stacey's arrival less than eight months after his parents wedding."

"I'd forgotten about that." Meli stepped back from the wardrobe, a powder pink day dress draped over her arm. "Poor Stacey. Can you imagine finding out the person you grew up believing was your father, wasn't?" She tilted her head, her eyes meeting Elizabeth's in the triptych mirror. "Do you think Sir Lionel knows?"

"He wouldn't be the first husband to raise another man's child to avoid a scandal." Elizabeth set the brush aside. "Men of his position often choose discretion over disgrace."

"But if he knows..." Meli's voice carried from behind the privacy screen. "That would give him motive, wouldn't it? All these years raising another man's child... Especially someone like Vale, who stands for everything Sir Lionel believes is wrong with modern society."

"To a man of Sir Lionel's standing, his reputation is everything." Elizabeth uncapped the gold tube, swiping a coat of rose-pink tint across her lips. "Although he strikes me as someone who'd use the law as his weapon of choice, rather than an artist's tool."

"I suppose." Meli emerged from behind the screen, her fingers fastening the pearl buttons running down the front of her dress. "But, I'm sure this is one case he'd want kept under wraps. Can you imagine the scandal?" She crossed to the dressing table, her fingers working through her long, dark curls, twisting and tucking while she studied her reflection in the mirror.

"Indeed." Elizabeth capped the lipstick tube with a soft click. "I've been thinking." She met Meli's eyes in the mirror. "I need to speak with Vivi again. She and Alice used to be close friends, she might know something about Stacey's paternity, perhaps even how much Sir Lionel knows."

"Mmm." Meli reached for a handful of pins and secured them between her teeth. She slid one into place, securing one rebellious curl, followed by another. "She might, but won't she find it odd? You're visiting her gallery again so soon?"

"I'll just have to find a way to bring it up naturally."

"I wish you luck." Meli pushed the final pin into place. "It's hardly the kind of thing one drops into casual conversation."

"True, but I'm sure I'll think of something."

The doorbell chime resonated along the landing.

Meli glanced at the mantel clock. "Ten on the dot. At least the Chief Inspector's punctual, if nothing else."

"Ready?" Elizabeth rose from the dressing table.

"As I'll ever be, but I could think of at least a dozen other ways I'd rather spend my morning than with the pompous Chief Inspector." She pulled the bedroom door closed behind them.

They made their way along the landing and down the stairs, Walsh's authoritative rumble rising from the sitting-room. Mrs Bramley's voice held that particular chill she reserved for unwelcome visitors – all politeness and ice as she offered refreshments.

They reached the bottom step as Mrs Bramley withdrew from the sitting-room, her mouth set in a thin line of disapproval.

"They're in the sitting-room, Lady Elizabeth." Mrs Bramley's hushed tones carried her indignation. "The way he's conducting himself, you'd think this was some common boarding house rather than a respectable home."

"Thank you, Mrs Bramley. Is Gigi with them?"

"Oh, you know Miss Gigi and her foreign ways, Lady Elizabeth. She'll be down when she's ready. Now I'd best see to his lordship's tea."

Elizabeth entered the sitting-room, pausing in the doorway. Chief Inspector Walsh stood with his back to the window, thumbs hooked beneath his lapels, while the young constable, whom Meli had charmed into joining her at the Palace Pier Tea Rooms, stood nearby, his hands folded behind his back.

"Ah, Lady Elizabeth." Walsh's gaze slid from her to Meli. "Miss Diomaros. No, Miss Hamilton-Smythe?"

A flush crept up the constable's neck when he spotted Meli, but he kept his counsel.

"She'll join us shortly." Elizabeth settled into the green armchair, with Meli taking the sofa. "I understand you wish to take our statements."

"Indeed." Walsh remained by the window. "Miss Diomaros, if you'd wait outside, I'll be speaking with each of you individually."

Meli's brows arched in Elizabeth's direction as she rose from the sofa and crossed the room.

"Close the door behind you, will you?"

Elizabeth bit the inside of her cheek as the door closed with a little more force than was strictly necessary.

"I won't beat about the bush, Lady Elizabeth. It's been brought to my attention that you've been conducting your own investigation into Mr Vale's death."

"I wouldn't exactly call it an investigation." Elizabeth held his gaze.

"No? Then what exactly would you call poking about crime scenes and questioning witnesses?" Walsh slipped his hands into his trouser pockets, rocking on the balls of his feet. "I've heard you see yourself as something of a detective."

"I was simply making a few discrete enquiries on behalf of a friend."

"Is that what you call it?" Walsh snorted. "Because in my borough, it's called obstruction of justice."

The constable shifted his weight, his eyes fixed on the knot in the wooden floorboards.

"Let me be very clear, Lady Elizabeth." Walsh rocked forward on his feet. "I don't care what your title is or how many murder cases you claim to have solved, but in Brighton, no one is above the law, no matter who their *friends* are."

"I can assure you, Chief Inspector." Elizabeth's fingers tightened on the arm of her chair. "I don't consider myself above the law."

"Don't you? Then perhaps you can explain why you were seen leaving Vale's studio after it had been sealed by police order?"

The constable's flush deepened as his gaze darted to Elizabeth, then back to the floor.

"I'm afraid I don't know what you mean."

"Constable Hartwell here tells me a young lady matching your description was spotted leaving the studio the morning after Vale's murder."

"I think your constable must be mistaken. I would imagine the pier was quite busy that morning, and no doubt dark-haired young women in summer frocks were in great supply."

He pulled out his notebook, flipping through several pages. "Let's begin with the night of the murder. You attended the exhibition at the Palace Pier, correct?"

"Correct."

"And you accompanied Mrs Marchant and Mr Pembroke upstairs when Vale's body was discovered?"

"Correct again, Chief Inspector."

"Tell me about Miss Baker's state of mind that evening."

Elizabeth chose her words with care. "I hardly think I'm–"

"You hardly think what? That a woman found standing over a corpse with the murder weapon in her hand might be guilty? Or do you subscribe to the notion that women are incapable of violence?"

"I believe in evidence, Chief Inspector. Not assumptions."

"Evidence?" Walsh's notebook snapped shut. "The evidence in this case is overwhelming, yet you refuse to see what's staring you in the face. Miss Baker was found at the scene with the victim's blood on her hands."

"Sometimes things aren't always what they seem."

"And sometimes, Lady Elizabeth, they are exactly what they seem." His hand swept her words away. "This is what's wrong with your generation – too much sympathy for criminals, not enough respect for law and order."

"Begging your pardon, sir." The constable cleared his throat. "But should I be writing this down, sir?"

"For heaven's sake, man..." The Chief Inspector pinched the bridge of his nose between his forefinger and thumb. "Just fetch the next one in, will you?"

Elizabeth rose from her chair, her shoulders rigid. "I assume I'm free to go?"

"For now." He fixed her with his steely gaze. "But let me be very clear, Lady Elizabeth. If I find you interfering in my investigation again,

I'll have you arrested, regardless of your ... connections."

"Of course, Chief Inspector." Elizabeth inclined her head.

Walsh folded his arms across his chest, smug satisfaction etched across his features as he watched her leave.

Elizabeth closed the sitting-room door behind her and drew in a slow breath.

If the Chief Inspector thought his threats had bullied her into ending her investigation ... then he had woefully underestimated her.

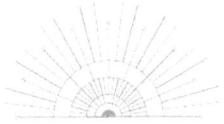

Chapter Sixteen

THE HOLIDAY CROWDS WERE beginning to gather along the Palace Pier as Elizabeth made her way towards the gallery – children clustered around the hoopla stalls, a group of day-trippers sampled pink wisps of candy floss and visitors perused the display of seaside postcards.

A break-in at Vale's studio had necessitated a change of plan. According to Vivi's assistant at the Western Road gallery, she'd departed for the pier thirty minutes prior to Elizabeth's arrival, summoned by an urgent telephone call from the police.

The Chief Inspector's warning rang in her ears as she climbed the wooden steps to Vale's studio. *If I find you interfering in my investigation again, I'll have you arrested, regardless of your ... connections.*

But it was hardly her fault if the Chief Inspector had mistaken her politeness for acquiescence, was it?

A young constable stepped forward, blocking her path as she reached the top step.

"I'm sorry, miss, but you can't come in here. Police business."

"Oh, it's quite all right, constable." Vivi appeared at his shoulder. "Lady Elizabeth is a friend."

The constable stepped aside, allowing Elizabeth entry.

"Please forgive the mess." Vivi shook her head at the disarray of bottles and supplies. "Though knowing Vale as I do–did, it's impossible to tell if this was just his usual mess, the aftermath of the police search or due to the break-in. But what can I do for you, Lady Elizabeth?"

"I called at your Western Road gallery. Your assistant told me what had happened." Elizabeth stepped between the discarded paint tubes and brushes littering the floor. "So I came to offer my assistance."

"That's very kind, but I wouldn't want to impose."

"It's no imposition, I assure you." Elizabeth's gaze swept the studio, searching for any changes since her previous visit. "Actually, I'm rather grateful for the excuse to avoid Chief Inspector Walsh. He's up at Adelaide Crescent taking statements."

"Did he, er..." Vivi's fingers curled around the dark green whisky bottle sitting amongst the mess. "Did Walsh mention anything about the postmortem results?"

Elizabeth watched Vivi's hand tighten around the bottle. What was her preoccupation with the postmortem results? And even more curious was the way she cradled that bottle ... the very one Elizabeth had detected the valerian in.

Had Vivi been dosing Vale's whisky?

"You know Walsh, but..." Elizabeth paused. "No, I shouldn't say."

Vivi's knuckles whitened against the green of the bottle. "Say what?"

"Well, between you and me." Elizabeth leaned in closer. "One of the constables let slip Vale had rather a high concentration of valerian in his system. A lethal amount, by all accounts."

SMASH!

The bottle slipped through Vivi's fingers, shattering against the floorboards.

"Let me help." Elizabeth crouched opposite Vivi while Vivi gathered the larger shards of glass in her hands.

"Please, you might cut yourself." Vivi's fingers hovered above the broken pieces.

Elizabeth sniffed the air, the sharp, earthy scent of valerian rising from the spillage.

Vivi stilled, her gaze meeting Elizabeth's.

"I never meant for any of this…"

Elizabeth straightened, pressing her finger to her lips as she assessed the constable's position. "We might be more comfortable away from the door." She indicated the far window, lowering her voice. "And less likely to be overheard."

Vivi nodded, following her lead as they crossed the studio.

"It's not what you think. I did it to protect Vale … to protect us both." Her hand brushed against the window frame, shoulders rising with a deep inhale. "When you asked me the other day about the artist you saw me talking to at the exhibition, I lied when I said I didn't remember him. He's an artist named Miles Fenner, or Fenn as he prefers to be known. He approached me after the sale to Sir Geoffrey became public, claiming Vale had stolen his work. At first, I thought he was a chancer, trying it on, so I ignored him."

Elizabeth listened in silence, noting each detail that aligned with Fenn's account.

"But then he brought photographs of the actual location." Vivi's voice dropped. "The painting Vale called *Tuscan Spring* wasn't Tuscany at all. The cathedral in the background was Orvieto, in Umbria. Any fool could see the differences once they were pointed out, but I'd been so eager to believe Vale's renaissance that I hadn't looked closely enough." She pressed her fingertips to her temples. "I felt such a complete fool."

"Did you confront Vale?"

"I had to. Sir Geoffrey Ward isn't just any collector – he sits on museum boards, moves in the highest circles. If word got out that I'd sold him stolen work…" Vivi's voice dropped. "But Vale laughed. Said if I breathed a word to Sir Geoffrey, he'd tell everyone I was complicit."

"He had me trapped." Vivi turned towards the window, arms wrapping around herself. "Criminal conspiracy charges could mean prison, but even without that, the scandal alone would destroy both my business and personal reputation. No respectable collector would ever trust me again."

"What about Fenn? Did you explain what would happen if word got out?"

"I tried. I offered to compensate him for his loss, not the full fifty guineas, of course. But he wasn't interested in money. He wanted recognition, wanted the art world to know the truth."

Elizabeth followed Vivi's gaze to the brightly attired holidaymakers dotting the pier like confetti below the window.

"I was caught in the middle … Vale threatening to destroy me if I spoke up, Fenn threatening to expose us both if I didn't make things right. So, I tried to buy some time by avoiding Fenn's messages, and hoped something might resolve itself."

"Is that what you and Fenn were arguing about at the exhibition?"

"I knew he might turn up and cause a scene. I tried to convince Vale to withdraw from the exhibition, pretend he was unwell and we could have re-scheduled, but that man is–" Vivi corrected herself. "Was so bloody-minded he was convinced Fenn wouldn't have the nerve to show up and spoil his big night. But I wasn't convinced, so I took matters into my own hands…"

Elizabeth had no proof, only instinct to go on, but sometimes the boldest move was the surest path to truth. "Is that why you gave him the valerian?"

"Yes…" Vivi's gaze darted between Elizabeth and the window, her words tumbling out in a rush. "I was desperate to prevent a public confrontation. I started slipping it into his whisky in the run-up to the exhibition. Only it wasn't working, so I kept adding more and more. When he died, I panicked. But I swear, I only wanted him ill enough to miss the show."

Vivi caught herself, the weight of her confession dawning. "You, er … you won't mention anything about the valerian to the police, will you, Lady Elizabeth?"

Elizabeth considered the implications. The valerian hadn't killed Vale; the pathologist's report had been clear on that point. Had Vivi continued increasing the dosage, however, the outcome might have been far more sinister. Not to mention what would happen if the Chief Inspector discovered she was withholding information after his explicit warning about interfering with his investigation, the consequences would be severe indeed.

"I won't volunteer the information to the police." Elizabeth met Vivi's anxious gaze. "But should I be asked directly, I won't lie."

"Of course, I understand." Vivi squared her shoulders, her smile forced and brittle. "I suppose I'd better make a start sorting through all this." She surveyed the studio, taking in the stacks of canvases propped against the walls, paint tubes and brushes scattered across every surface, empty jam jars lying on their sides. "The police want me to identify anything that might have been taken during the break-in, though where one even begins…"

"I could help, if you like," Elizabeth offered. "After all, four eyes are better than two, and we'll get through it all in half the time."

"That's very kind, but how would you know what to look for?"

"I had the opportunity to have a quick look around on the night of Vale's mur–the exhibition, while we waited for the police to arrive."

"In that case, I would be glad of an extra pair of eyes and hands."

Elizabeth's gaze swept the space. "Have the police mentioned who they think might be responsible? Or what they were looking for?"

"They've told me hardly anything. Just asked me to come down and have a look around." Vivi's attention caught on Vale's mattress, now rolled clear of the canvas stack that had concealed it during Elizabeth's previous visit.

"Did you know he was living here?"

"I suspected as much, but he always denied it whenever I brought it up." Vivi turned to the nearest stack of canvases. "Would you mind taking that side, and I'll search through these? Though heaven knows who'd break in just to steal artwork. It's not as if he was one of the Masters."

"Fenn?" The word slipped out unbidden

"Why would Fenn break in?" Vivi frowned at the suggestion. "It's not as if his painting is here."

"Perhaps he thought Vale might have stolen others." Elizabeth kept her voice light.

"I suppose you might be right." Vivi returned to the canvases, while Elizabeth worked her way through her own stack.

"Well, well…" Vivi traced the edge of a canvas with her thumb. "Now here's something from another lifetime."

"What is it?"

"Alice Ellis." Vivi lifted a small canvas. "Stacey's mother."

Elizabeth stepped closer, her eyes instantly drawn to the figure reclining against a bed of emerald silk, a whisper of rose chiffon draped across her body. Her black hair spilled loose against pale skin, and she gazed at the artist, her head tilted slightly, the faintest smile playing at the corner of her lips.

"Breathtaking, wasn't she?"

"She was indeed. Stacey bears a striking resemblance to her."

"She could have had any man in Brighton, you know." Vivi shook her head. "Such a shame she only had eyes for the wrong ones … first Vale, then Sir Lionel." She paused, studying the portrait. "I never understood how she could just leave Stacey like that. Not a word in all these years."

"How old was she when this was painted?"

Vivi studied the painting, her head angled to one side. "It was after young Stacey was born; you can tell by that ghastly ring she's wearing. Sir Lionel had it made to commemorate the birth, with a peridot at its centre to mark August. Alice hated it, but he insisted she wear it." Vivi shook her head, her mouth twisting. "The irony was, Stacey arrived in July, yet Sir Lionel refused to change the stone."

The ring, Alice's ring, was the same one Rosalind had been wearing in her painting. No wonder Sir Lionel had reacted so peculiarly.

I wonder? Had Essie also been wearing Alice's ring when she'd posed for her own portrait, just as Rosalind and Alice had?

Elizabeth returned to the stack of canvases, flicking through each one before starting over.

"I think I know what's missing. It's one of the *Nymphaeum* paintings."

"Are you sure?" Vivi's brow creased. "Who on earth would risk breaking in just to steal one of those?"

Who indeed?

Two possibilities crystallised in Elizabeth's mind.

Laurence Pembroke.

And Essie herself.

"Chief Inspector's here, ma'am," the constable called from the doorway as Walsh's footsteps echoed on the stairs.

Elizabeth's breath hitched. If Walsh found her here…

She glanced at the window, recalling Fenn's escape route across the rooftops.

Elizabeth pushed up the sash and swung one leg over the sill as she turned to Vivi. "I was never here."

Chapter Seventeen

A CHARABANC RATTLED ALONG Kings Road below, its benches crowded with sun-pinked day-trippers bound for the station. A man's voice rose above the engine, tuneless but cheerful, and was quickly joined by others, their chorus drifting in through the open bedroom window.

Meli twisted another curl into place and reached for a pin. "I'm going to miss this evening chorus when we're back in London." She turned toward the window as the singing swelled. "Everyone sounds so jolly."

"Indeed, they do. There's something about the sea air that lifts the spirits." Elizabeth stepped out from behind the privacy screen.

"Would you mind helping with these buttons? My shoulder's a little tender."

"I'm not surprised." Meli's fingers worked to secure the buttons on Elizabeth's Jeanne Lanvin gown of soft wisteria silk chiffon, its sheer overlay cinched at the hip with embroidered violets. "What were you thinking scrambling over rooftops like a cat burglar just to avoid the Chief Inspector? What if you'd fallen?"

"Needs must when the devil drives, as they say." Elizabeth met her cousin's eyes in the mirror. "Though I doubt my knees will thank me for it. Or my stockings." She gestured ruefully to the laddered silks draped across the end of her bed. "Still, at least I had the foresight to remove my shoes beforehand."

Meli's mouth parted in disbelief. "You could have broken your neck, and you're worried about torn stockings and scuffed shoes?"

"Grazed knees mend soon enough. Scuffed Perugia's, on the other hand, are a tragedy." Elizabeth eased herself onto the dressing table stool with a groan. "Though I confess, it's not something I'm eager to repeat."

"I'm very glad to hear it." Meli reached for her jewellery case and selected a single silver filigree earring, turning it in the light before fastening it to her lobe. "Speaking of close calls, what do you make of Vivi's confession about the valerian? Do you really believe she was only trying to incapacitate Vale?"

Elizabeth paused, lipstick poised mid-air as she considered Meli's words. "Vale's unsteadiness at the exhibition was attributed to drink, but it could just as easily have been because of the valerian. And the rest of her story aligns with Fenn's, which gives weight to both. Unless the two of them agreed on their story in advance."

"But Fenn has a watertight alibi for the time of the murder, remember?"

"True, but an alibi doesn't guarantee innocence," Elizabeth countered. "The pier was crowded that evening, and time can become more fluid when one's on holiday. Fenn could have met the women later than he claimed. We know he had the skill to slip into the studio unnoticed, even with the constable guarding the front door, and he certainly had motive enough for revenge ... but whether he had the time is the question."

Meli lowered herself beside Elizabeth, turning her head to admire the earring in the mirror. "Do you think Fenn was behind the break-in last night?"

"I did briefly, after the last time. But since Essie's painting is the only thing missing, that points to either Pembroke or Essie herself."

"Essie? Slipping out of the house and breaking into Vale's studio in the dead of night?" Meli shook her head. "I just don't see it."

"No, I can't see it either. Which brings us back to Pembroke."

"Surely he wouldn't be that reckless, not with the elections just around the corner."

"Indeed. But money has a way of finding willing hands." Elizabeth met Meli's eyes in the mirror, an eyebrow arched. "And I imagine his work in prison reform brings him into contact with all manner of characters – some better suited to shadows than sunlight."

"I hadn't thought of that." Meli fumbled with the clip on the second earring. "Would you mind? I'm all fingers and thumbs."

She dipped her head while Elizabeth fastened the clasp.

"Was she really as beautiful as people say ... Alice, I mean?"

"Very much so. Stacey's just like her – he has the same features and colouring."

"I simply cannot fathom it." Meli shook her head. "How could any mother abandon her child? Whatever happened between her and Sir Lionel, how could she leave her son behind?"

"Perhaps she felt she had no alternative. Sir Lionel is a wealthy man with considerable influence. A High Court judge with connections throughout the legal system. What chance would Alice have had of securing custody? The courts almost invariably favour the father, particularly one of Sir Lionel's standing."

"I hadn't considered that. Though I can't imagine why anyone would marry Sir Lionel in the first place. That man exudes all the warmth of a January frost."

Elizabeth selected a marcasite hair comb with a striking geometric design from the velvet-lined tray in her dressing case and slid it into place. "I suspect she may not have had much choice in that matter either."

A knock at the door interrupted their conversation.

"Come in," Meli called.

Lily hovered in the doorway. "Miss Gigi says the taxi's waiting, my ladies."

"Thank you, Lily. Tell her we'll be down shortly." Elizabeth rose from the dressing table and gathered her evening bag while Meli checked her reflection one final time.

"Here, let me–" Meli offered her arm as Elizabeth made her way towards the door, her movements measured.

"Thank you, but I'm quite all right. Just a little stiff, that's all."

Meli turned off the lights before pulling the door closed behind them.

Gigi and Essie waited in the entrance hall, Gigi with one hand on her hip. "And here I thought I was the only one who kept to Italian time." She glanced up as Elizabeth and Meli descended the stairs.

"It was my fault." Meli's fingers brushed the pearl beading at her hip where the shell-pink georgette gathered into a soft drape. "I couldn't decide which dress to wear."

"Then you're forgiven." Gigi's lips curved into a smile. "Every girl wants to look her best, and that gown is perfect on you." She reached for the doorknob and yanked open the front door. "Shall we?"

They made their way down the front steps, to where the taxi idled beyond the communal gardens. Essie slid in first, gathering the folds of her champagne silk gown as she settled into her seat. Meli followed, then Elizabeth. Gigi climbed in last, smoothing the handkerchief hem of her turquoise chiffon over her knees as she pulled the door shut.

The driver glanced over his shoulder. "Where to tonight, ladies?"

"Number fourteen Sussex Square, if you please," Gigi replied.

The taxi pulled away from Adelaide Crescent, slipping onto Kings Road where the last evening strollers made their way along Hove Lawns. The terraces soon gave way to Brunswick Square's grand facades, its gardens glimpsed through wrought iron and clipped hedges. Along Western Road, shopkeepers drew down their blinds while tea rooms filled with evening patrons.

At Montpelier, the taxi swung north past a leafy park before easing east, where Regency townhouses lined the quieter streets. Sussex Square came into view as a broad crescent of creamy stucco, set back from the road in orderly rows, behind neat privet hedges and formal gardens.

Outside number fourteen, the driver slowed to a halt.

Elizabeth braced against the taxi's door frame as she alighted, her descent slow and laboured.

"Still sore?" Gigi counted coins into the driver's palm. "I can't believe you tripped over a Pekingese. You're usually so sure-footed."

"You know how these small dogs are, always darting between one's ankles."

They'd barely reached the top step when the door opened. A butler appeared, his morning coat and striped trousers a study in starched propriety.

"Good evening, ladies. This way, if you please." He closed the door behind them.

Meli's fingers brushed Elizabeth's arm as they trailed the others. "A Pekingese?"

"A harmless little fib when Gigi caught me limping into the kitchen earlier." Elizabeth kept her voice low. "It seemed preferable to explaining about the Chief Inspector and Essie's painting."

"Lady Elizabeth, Miss Hamilton-Smythe, Miss Baker and Miss Diomaros," the butler announced as they entered the drawing-room.

"We'd almost given up on you." Stacey crossed to greet them. "Though with Gigi involved, I suppose we should have added another half hour to the expected arrival time."

"I'll have you know we're on time by Tuscan standards." Gigi swept past him.

"I'll see to the drinks, thank you, Wilson." Stacey moved to the sideboard.

"Very good, sir." The butler inclined his head before withdrawing.

"What's everyone having? Gigi, Essie, the usual?"

"Please." Gigi settled herself beside Sylvia on the sofa.

"And what about you, Meli?"

"I'll have a gin rickey, please, with plenty of soda water."

"Lady Elizabeth?"

"Just water for me, thank you."

"Are you sure I can't get you something else?" Stacey paused, bottle in hand.

"Positive, I can feel one of my headaches coming on."

"Can I get you something for it? An aspirin perhaps, or something stronger? My father's medicine cabinet is better stocked than any chemist's in Brighton."

"Thank you, but I'm sure it will pass soon enough if I just sit here quietly." Elizabeth caught Meli's questioning look and gave a small shake of her head.

"Talking of Sir Lionel, where is he tonight? Will he be joining us for dinner along with his disapproving scowl?" Rosalind asked.

"He's in London on court business." Stacey moved between the guests, distributing their drinks. "Won't be back until tomorrow."

"That's something to be grateful for then." Rosalind held up her glass in a toast. " I do so hate gulping down good gin just to remind him he's your father, not mine."

Tommy's gaze flicked to Stacey, then back to Rosalind. "Have you all heard the latest about Rosalind's tumble the other night? She's convinced someone tried to kill her."

"I never said someone was trying to kill me, for heaven's sake." Rosalind drew on her cigarette, blowing smoke from the corner of her mouth. "All I said was, someone pushed me down the stairs. You can mock all you want, Tommy Cavendish, but I know what I felt."

"Gigi, remind me again about the serpent bite that almost claimed Rosalind's life in Tuscany last summer." Tommy's gaze slid to Rosalind as he paused for effect. "But hang on, didn't the deadly assailant turn out to be … an ant?"

"*Dio mio*, what a performance!" Gigi's hands flew up in perfect imitation. "Doctor Vannini had thrown up his hands and said he'd seen women delivering twins make less fuss than *l'inglesina*."

"You forced me to trek to that wretched little village." Rosalind's cigarette jabbed the air.

"Trek? Hardly. It's barely a twenty-minute stroll when wearing the appropriate footwear."

Rosalind fluttered her fingers through the smoke, as if brushing away such practicality. "If God had intended one to trek through the wilderness, he wouldn't have invented hand-stitched soles, would he?"

"Oh, vanity, thy name is footwear." Markus raised his glass.

Tommy leaned back against the mantel, satisfaction playing across his features. "And therein I rest my case."

"What does *l'inglesina* mean?" Sylvia asked.

"Roughly translated." Essie's gaze found Rosalind's. "I believe it means … fussy Englishwoman."

Against the burst of laughter, Rosalind's eyes narrowed at Essie as she took a long, deliberate draw on her cigarette.

Wilson announced his arrival with a discrete cough. "Dinner is served, sir."

As the others filed into the dining-room, Elizabeth pressed her fingers to her temple, swaying slightly as she rose.

"Elizabeth?" Meli caught her arm.

"I think I must have stood up too quickly." Elizabeth steadied herself against the sofa.

"Here, you'd better sit down." Stacey took her other arm. "Before you fall down."

"I'm so sorry to be such a nuisance." Elizabeth sank onto the sofa. "Would it be terribly rude of me to miss dinner? Perhaps if I sat here..."

"Nonsense. You need to rest properly," Stacey said. "We have plenty of guest rooms upstairs."

"Oh, I couldn't impose–"

"It's no imposition at all." Stacey turned towards the door. "I'll have Wilson arrange for one of the maids to show you upstairs."

"I'll stay with you," Meli offered as Stacey left the room.

"Absolutely not." Elizabeth kept her voice low. "I need you to be my eyes and ears down here, while I have a look around upstairs."

"But what if Sir Lionel catches you?"

"He's in London until tomorrow, remember?"

"Was this your plan all along?"

"Begging your pardon, my lady." A maid stood in the doorway. "If you'll follow me, I'll show you to your room."

Elizabeth rose.

With no new leads and all the evidence painting Essie as the murderer, Elizabeth needed to cast her net a little wider, and a name that kept coming up was Alice Grimwald.

They had only Sir Lionel's word that Alice had left for America all those years ago, and a man of means and influence could easily orchestrate the banishment of an inconvenient wife.

Perhaps Sir Lionel had a forwarding address or letters hidden away that might hint at Alice's whereabouts.

Alice had motive enough to want Vale dead.

If Sir Lionel found out he wasn't Stacey's father, Stacey could lose everything.

But would a mother really go as far as to commit murder for her child?

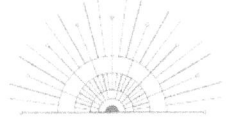

Chapter Eighteen

ELIZABETH FOLLOWED THE MAID up the staircase. A line of portraits marked their progress, men in judicial robes and horsehair wigs, each bearing the unmistakable Grimwald features. At the top, the landing revealed a collection of gilded frames. In one, a young Stacey stood beside his father, small shoulders squared, his mother's features softened by childhood.

"Here you are, my lady." The maid opened the third door. The room was decorated in shades of green, from the silk-striped wallpaper to the heavy damask curtains. A mahogany bed dominated one wall, its covers neatly turned down. "Would you like me to bring you anything, my lady? Perhaps some tea, or a cool cloth for your head?"

"No, thank you." Elizabeth's fingers brushed her temple as she perched on the corner of the bed. "I'm sure I'll be right as rain after a rest."

"Very good, my lady. If you change your mind, the bell pull is next to the bed."

Elizabeth waited until the maid's footsteps faded into silence. She eased the door open, peering through the gap up and down the landing.

Elizabeth crept along the landing, keeping close to the wall. She paused at each door, pressing her ear to the wood, listening before knocking. When no response came, she eased open the door. Behind the first lay Stacey's bedroom, the second another guest room – a mirror of her own in blue rather than green.

The third door was locked. Elizabeth glanced along the landing once more before withdrawing two hairpins from her bag. She worked them into the lock until it surrendered with a click, then slipped inside.

Dark oak furniture filled the space – twin wardrobes, a leather armchair by the fireplace, a cheval mirror, and a bureau against the far wall. The brass clock on the mantel marked each second. Only Sir Lionel would keep a room with such rigid order.

Elizabeth froze at the sound of approaching footsteps, her heart racing as they came to a halt outside the door. A key scraped in the lock while she searched for an escape. The doorknob rattled. If it were one of the staff, she could explain her presence as a simple mistake. But what if it was Sir Lionel, returned early from London...

Elizabeth's glance flew from the bed to the curtains. The key turned a second time, and she made a dash for the window, pressing herself behind the heavy fabric as the door opened.

The mirror afforded Elizabeth a clear view as Sir Lionel made his way to the writing bureau, his movements betraying an unfamiliar weariness. Each breath seemed to cost him effort as he flattened his palms against the polished surface and lowered himself into the chair. As he switched on the electric lamp, the brightness spilled across the desk, illuminating the white gauze wrapped around his right hand. Her fingers found the small scab on her palm from her stumble on Vale's studio steps.

Sir Lionel reached into his waistcoat pocket, withdrawing a small key that glinted as he unlocked a concealed compartment within the bureau. From its depths, he withdrew a tattered notebook, its leather binding worn at the corners, pages yellowed with age. He thumbed through the pages until he found his place, then uncapped his pen and dipped it into the waiting ink bottle before scribbling something on the pages. Elizabeth watched as he pressed blotting paper against the fresh ink, then crumpled it before dropping it into his wastebasket.

He reached into the compartment once more, drawing out a small object. He held it to the light, examining it between his thumb and forefinger. Elizabeth's eyes narrowed as she squinted into the mirror ... was that Alice's ring?

Sir Lionel braced his elbows against the desk and buried his head in his hands. Seconds stretched into minutes before he stirred. Closing the notebook, he returned both items to their hiding place. He slipped the key back into his waistcoat pocket after securing the compartment, his movements slow and deliberate as he capped his pen.

He took a moment before pushing himself up from the chair, one hand pressed against the desk for support. Drawing himself to his full height, he inhaled deeply, then left the room, the key turning in the lock behind him.

Elizabeth's shoulders dropped, the tension ebbing as she stepped out from behind the curtain. She reached into the wastebasket for Sir Lionel's discarded paper. As she withdrew it, another scrunched-up ball caught her eye, wedged behind one of the bureau's legs and barely visible in the shadow. Elizabeth dropped to her hands and knees, working her arm into the narrow gap between the bureau and the wall. Her fingertips brushed the paper's edge, then coaxed it forward until she could grasp it properly.

She smoothed the crumpled papers against the bureau's surface, her eyes narrowing at Sir Lionel's angular scrawl. On the recent sheet, two names were written in black ink, one with a Latin inscription beside it. The older page held three names, each with its own Latin text flowing alongside. Her elbow knocked the ink bottle as she leaned across to examine the names more closely.

Elizabeth swept both sheets clear of the bureau as black ink crept across the surface. Her fingers found the blotting pad, tearing off sheet after sheet to contain the spread. She pressed each fresh sheet down, lifting away the dark liquid until the pad grew thin. She reached into her bag for her cotton handkerchief, rubbing at the wood grain until all trace of the ink was gone.

She wrapped the ink-stained blotting sheets in her handkerchief, grimacing at the dark seepage already colouring the silk lining of her bag. Folding the other two sheets, she slipped them into a separate compartment.

Elizabeth stepped back from the bureau, her eyes sweeping the room to ensure nothing betrayed her presence. Satisfied, she retrieved the two hairpins from her bag and worked at the lock until it yielded, checking the landing in both directions before exiting.

Elizabeth hurried along the landing from Sir Lionel's bedroom, slowing as she spotted the guest bedroom door ajar.

"Oh, my lady." The maid's hand flew to her chest. "Mr Eustace asked me to see if you were feeling better or needed anything."

"I'm much better, thank you." *How long had she been here?* "I'd just been in search of the bathroom."

"It's at the end of the–"

"It's all right, I found it."

"Are you feeling well enough to join the others, my lady? They've moved to the drawing-room."

"I am indeed." Elizabeth followed her downstairs to the drawing-room, where conversation centred on Sir Lionel's unexpected arrival.

"Elizabeth!" Gigi set down her glass. "Are you feeling any better?"

"Much improved, thank you." Elizabeth settled into one of the armchairs. "Though I suspect an early night would be wise."

Rosalind tapped her cigarette against the side of a crystal ashtray. "Sir Lionel's return has ensured an early night for everyone."

Gigi leaned forward in her seat, her hand brushing Elizabeth's arm. "I hope you don't mind, but I've asked Wilson to call for a taxi. I thought it best to get you home."

"Surely you're not all leaving?" Stacey returned to the drawing-room. "It's not even nine o'clock."

"I thought it best we leave, since Elizabeth is unwell." Gigi shifted in her chair, her fingers adjusting the chiffon of her skirt. "And Wilson's already arranged our taxi."

"But the rest of you…" Stacey turned to the others.

"Sorry, but I have an early start in the morning." Sylvia rose from the sofa.

Rosalind ground her cigarette into the crystal ashtray, her lips curving in a feline smile. "For once, that dreary little job of yours serves a purpose."

"Excuse me, Mr Eustace." Wilson stood at the threshold of the drawing-room. "Miss Hamilton-Smythe's taxi has arrived."

"We might as well all leave at the same time." Rosalind uncoiled from the armchair.

"We wouldn't want to keep Sylvia up past her bedtime, now would we?"

The group spilled into the entrance hall. "Careful on the front steps, Rosalind." Tommy's voice dropped to a stage whisper. "I hear the roses are simply crawling with deadly assassins."

"Don't even joke about it, Tommy." Rosalind paled. "You know I'm deathly allergic to bees."

"Always has to be the centre of attention." Tommy rolled his eyes, sweeping Rosalind off her feet in one fluid movement. "Never fear! I'll protect you from the killer swarm!"

"Bees don't come out after dark, you ridiculous fool." Rosalind's laughter ricocheted around the hallway as Tommy carried her down the front steps with exaggerated care. Marcus and Sylvia called their goodnights to Stacey over their shoulders as they trailed behind them.

Gigi squeezed Stacey's hand. "Dinner was delicious, wouldn't you agree, ladies?"

Meli and Essie echoed their agreement as they descended the front steps to the waiting taxi.

"Thank you for your kindness tonight." Elizabeth rested a hand on Stacey's arm. His earlier thoughtfulness sharpening her guilt over her deception.

"Not at all." Stacey's shoulders lifted in a half shrug. "I'm just sorry you were not well enough to continue our evening."

"Good night ... Lady Elizabeth." Elizabeth's attention snapped to the top of the stairs, her gaze locking with Sir Lionel's icy stare.

After what felt like minutes, he inclined his head, turning his back on her as he disappeared from view.

Her fingers flexed against Stacey's arm, her eyes drawn to the black ink staining her skin.

Elizabeth swallowed hard.

Had Sir Lionel spotted the ink stain on her hand? Did he know what she'd done?

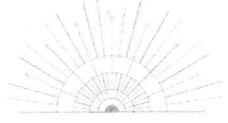

Chapter Nineteen

ELIZABETH ROLLED HER SHOULDERS, every muscle protesting her scramble across Brighton's rooftops the day before. The ink stain on her thumb caught her eye as she lifted her teacup, Sir Lionel's words echoing in her mind. That pointed "Good night ... Lady Elizabeth". Had it been his subtle way of letting her know he was aware of her presence in his bedroom? She'd tried to read the reversed writing on the blotting paper after they'd returned home the previous evening, but exhaustion and blurred vision had driven her to her bed.

"That boy gets later every morning." Mrs Bramley bustled into the morning-room, balancing her silver tray in her hands, setting down The Times, a fresh pot of tea, and fresh toast.

"I'll have to have a word, or he'll be delivering the morning paper with the evening edition at this rate." Her eyes lingered on Elizabeth's empty plate. "You're looking a mite peaky this morning, Lady Elizabeth, if you don't mind my saying. Shall I fetch you some eggs? A bit of kedgeree, perhaps?"

Elizabeth lifted her chin from where it had been resting against her palm. "Tea is perfectly fine, thank you, Mrs Bramley."

"It's no bother; I can make something up in a tick."

"No, really … just the tea will do."

Essie reached for the fresh pot. "Meli?"

"Please." Meli held out her cup.

Elizabeth and Gigi shook their heads at Essie's questioning glance.

"There's nothing like a good cup of tea, sets the world right again, as my old mum used to say," Mrs Bramley said.

"That's what Papa says." Gigi drizzled a spoonful of honey onto her toast. "Despite embracing most things Italian, he refuses to give up his afternoon Darjeeling."

"Ah yes, your father wouldn't miss his afternoon cuppa for anything." Mrs Bramley gathered the empty plates. "Four o'clock on the dot. Not a minute after."

"Afternoon tea is the only civilised ritual this modern age hasn't destroyed yet," Gigi said, mimicking Aunt Beatrice's precise tones.

"Now, Miss Gigi, that's no way to speak of such a fine lady as Lady Hawthorne." Mrs Bramley's reproach held no real sting.

"You're quite right, Mrs B, and I apologise." Gigi inclined her head, a ghost of a smile playing on her lips.

"Yes, well, we'll say no more about it. But her ladyship's right about the modern age." Mrs Bramley nodded towards The Times. "I know one shouldn't speak ill of the dead, but I can't say I'm sorry. Four wives drowned on their honeymoon, and now he's been found dead in his own bath. And him a man of the cloth. The Lord does indeed work in mysterious ways."

Elizabeth turned the newspaper towards her and began reading.

HONEYMOON CASE CLERGYMAN FOUND DEAD IN BATH

The Rev. Thomas Brown, who resigned his benefice earlier this year following allegations concerning the deaths of four successive wives while abroad on honeymoon, was yesterday discovered dead in the bathroom of a lodging-house in Worthing. The body was found partially submerged...

Thomas Brown. Elizabeth's teacup stilled halfway to her lips. *T. Brown*. Of course, no wonder it sounded familiar.

"Speaking of Aunt Beatrice." Elizabeth pushed back her chair. "I should write to reassure her we haven't given up afternoon tea for cocktails."

Elizabeth climbed the stairs as fast as her aching muscles would allow, the newspaper story turning over in her mind. Once inside her bedroom, she crossed to the dressing table, where the blotting paper had sat since the previous night. She held up the most recent sheet to the mirror; the reversed reflection reading T. Brown, alongside some words in Latin. On the line below was Delilah – a single name without explanation.

"Is everything all right?" Meli entered. "You left in such a hurry, I was worried something was wrong."

"It was the story in the newspaper." Elizabeth lowered the blotting paper. "The clergyman, Thomas Brown, his name's here on Sir Lionel's papers."

"Which means it must be in his private notebook?" Meli joined Elizabeth at the dressing table. "How peculiar."

"If only I could translate these Latin phrases…" Elizabeth gestured at the mirror. "It might explain why they are in there."

"Shall I take a look?"

"You? I didn't know you read Latin?"

"My mother insisted I study the basics." Meli rolled her eyes. "So, when I marry a *nice* Greek doctor, I can assist with his prescriptions."

Elizabeth opened the dressing-table drawer, retrieving two sheets of paper. Meli curled into the teal velvet armchair by the window, using a book from the bedside table as a makeshift writing surface.

"Ready?" Elizabeth held the page up to the mirror.

Meli copied down the letters as Elizabeth read aloud.

"Rev Thomas Brown." Meli read from her notes. "*In tempore opportuno invenient eum aquae multae*. Which means, in a time of opportunity, the great waters shall come upon him."

"Seems rather apt, considering he drowned four wives."

"Nothing else for Delilah?" Meli looked up.

"No, that's it." Elizabeth reached for the second sheet of blotting paper.

"N. Greaves." Meli paused over the Latin. "*Qui gladio ferit, gladio perit*. He who wounds with the sword, perishes by the sword." She glanced up. "Is that name familiar?"

"No, it's not ringing any bells."

"B. Catchpole. *Scitote quod peccatum vestrum inveniet vos*." Meli worked through the Latin. "Know that your sin will find you out."

"Catchpole. Now that's a name I do recognise. He set fire to his house a couple of years ago. His wife and children died in their beds. The police never found him."

"M. Cray. *Qui arant iniquitatem et seminant malitiam, metent eam.* They who plough iniquity and sow wickedness shall reap it."

Five names. Four citations. Four judgements.

But what did it mean?

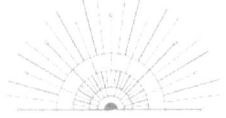

Chapter Twenty

ELIZABETH GUIDED GIGI'S VAUXHALL through the side gate of Adelaide Crescent onto Kings Road, where the June heat had drawn half of Brighton to the seafront. Sunlight glinted off the bonnets of touring cars as they crawled bumper to bumper, while children darted between vehicles clutching bathing costumes, and visitors lingered on the pavement to breathe in the sea air. Meli lurched forward as Elizabeth slammed on the brakes when a man in a straw boater stepped into their path, his newspaper raised against the glare.

"Sorry." Elizabeth flexed her fingers on the steering wheel.

"I daresay Brighton Library will still be standing whether we arrive in ten minutes or fifteen." Meli adjusted her hat. "We, on the other hand..."

"Yes, you're right ... sorry." Elizabeth eased the Vauxhall up a gear as the traffic inched forward.

"Do you really think Sir Lionel could be connected to Reverend Brown's death?" Meli twisted in her seat to face Elizabeth.

"I can't be certain, but Sir Lionel's mention of Brown's name in his notebook, the citation and discovery of the body ... it's all rather peculiar, don't you think?" Elizabeth pressed her foot to the accelerator as the traffic flowed more freely. "We know Sir Lionel's been away, but what if he hadn't been in London? Worthing's less than fifteen miles along the coast by motorcar; he could have been there and back in a matter of hours."

"But when you saw Sir Lionel last night in his bedroom, you said he seemed unwell, weakened." Meli's brow furrowed. "Would someone in that state have the strength to drown a man?"

"Given the right motivation, people can summon extraordinary strength." Elizabeth steered around a group of startled pigeons taking flight.

"Besides, drowning someone in a bath isn't about brute force; it's more about leverage and the element of surprise."

"Do you think he had anything to do with Vale's murder?" Meli kept her voice low.

"I believe he was in Vale's studio that night." Elizabeth guided the Vauxhall past the Royal Pavilion's gates. "Vale had possession of Alice's ring; we know that because Rosalind wore it for her portrait. And you saw Sir Lionel's reaction when he spotted it in the painting, how he pressed Rosalind about its whereabouts." She took the corner onto Church Street. "After leaving the gallery, I suspect he went to Vale's studio to retrieve it. That would explain his injured hand; he must have caught it on the same section of guardrail where I injured mine. The question is whether he went there simply to recover the ring … or for something more sinister."

"Shouldn't we tell the Chief Inspector?"

"He and Sir Lionel have known each other for years." Elizabeth cast a quick glance at Meli before returning her attention to the road ahead. "They belong to the same clubs, move in the same circles. I doubt the Chief Inspector would pursue any investigation without absolute proof ... and even then, I'm not so sure he'd act against him."

"But that's–" Meli broke off, her expression darkening. "So even the police protect their own."

Elizabeth eased the Vauxhall into a space near the library steps. "Let's not jump to any conclusions. I do, however, think the newspaper archives might shed some light on the other names on Sir Lionel's list."

Entering the library, they followed the corridor signs to the reference section, where grammar school boys and solicitors' clerks filled the tables, turning through newspapers and council records as they scribbled in their notebooks.

A librarian glanced up from her desk as they approached. "May I help you?"

"We'd like to consult your newspaper archives, if we may." Elizabeth kept her voice low. "The Brighton Gazette and Sussex Daily News."

"Of course." The librarian rose from her desk. "Which dates?"

"The last six months, if you would." Elizabeth glanced at Meli. "Though we may need to look further back."

The librarian nodded and disappeared into the archive room, returning with two bound volumes. "Take the desk by the window. Pencils only, please."

Elizabeth took one volume while Meli took the other, their eyes combing the column inches for any mention of the names on Sir Lionel's list.

"Elizabeth, listen to this," Meli read in hushed tones.

The Honourable Rosalind Delacourt caused quite a stir at Vale's exhibition, Meli read in hushed tones. *When asked about his daughter's rather modern portrait, Lord Delacourt, the 12th Baron of Wescombe, declined to comment, though if rumours are to be believed, perhaps it is Mr Justice Grimwald whose opinion should be sought."*

Meli showed the photograph beside the article; the same one used in Mrs Drummond-Ward's *About Town* column, showing Rosalind and Stacey at The Lux.

Elizabeth angled her head for a better view of the photograph.

"If Sir Lionel was feeling under the weather before, he'll be positively green around the gills after reading this," Meli said.

"Indeed. Rosalind isn't quite the daughter-in-law Sir Lionel pictured for the Grimwald name, I'm sure."

Elizabeth turned back to her volume, scanning the columns.

"Here ... Nathaniel Greaves." Elizabeth's finger traced beneath the headline. "A factory owner in Crawley. Three of his workers died in separate accidents involving a faulty grain press between 1916 and 1922. He was never prosecuted despite the inquest recommendations." She paused. "Then three weeks ago, they found him crushed beneath the same press."

"Qui gladio ferit, gladio perit," Meli read from Sir Lionel's list. "He who wounds with the sword, perishes by the sword."

They returned to their volumes, the rustle of pages the only sound between them.

"Bernard Catchpole," Meli whispered. "His wife and children died in a house fire in 1923. Two witnesses saw him set the fire and flee. They found petrol at the scene, but he disappeared before they could arrest him." She looked up. "Last month, his body was discovered in a burned-out shed. The police report mentions evidence of an accelerant."

"And here's Matilda Cray, an unlicensed midwife." Elizabeth's voice tightened. "A woman who helped desperate girls in trouble. Two died, including the daughter of a prominent family. She escaped prosecution when no one would testify." Elizabeth stopped, her eyes meeting Meli's. "They found her body eight days ago. She'd bled out from injuries that matched the wounds she allegedly inflicted on her victims."

"*Qui arant iniquitatem et seminant malitiam, metent eam*," Meli read. "They who plough iniquity and sow wickedness shall reap it."

"These deaths…" Elizabeth leaned closer to Meli across the desk. "Each one follows Sir Lionel's Latin judgments almost to the letter."

"A factory owner crushed by his own machine, an arsonist burned alive, and now this midwife…" Meli's hand stilled on the blotting paper. "But what about Delilah? There's no citation, no judgment…"

Of course! "Because she hasn't met her fate yet."

"Elizabeth, we must show this to Chief Inspector Walsh. Sir Lionel's notebook, these deaths ... it can't be mere coincidence. And what about Delilah? What if Sir Lionel–"

"We don't even know who she is. If we go to the Chief Inspector now with this list and a theory, he'll laugh us all the way down to the holding cells. These names…" Elizabeth's fingers brushed the blotting paper. "We could have copied them from anywhere. What we need is the notebook itself."

"Surely, you're not suggesting we return to Sir Lionel's house? Not after everything we've just discovered about him?"

"We don't have a choice."

"Elizabeth, I don't think…" The newspaper pages slipped through Meli's fingers, falling open on the photograph of Rosalind and Stacey at The Lux.

Elizabeth's chest tightened, her gaze flicking from the photograph to Meli.

"I ... I think I know who Delilah is."

Chapter Twenty-One

THE COLD WEIGHT OF Delilah's identity pressed against Elizabeth's chest, despite the June heat. Rosalind was Delilah, she was sure of it. And Sir Lionel had marked her for death.

"You don't think Sir Lionel–" Meli's voice caught.

"Brown, Greaves, Catchpole, Cray. Even Vale, perhaps." Elizabeth pushed back from the desk. "We need to find a telephone and warn her."

Elizabeth crossed to the librarian's desk, Meli close on her heels. "Excuse me, but do you have a telephone I might use?"

The librarian peered over her wire-rimmed spectacles. "I'm afraid the telephone is for library business only."

"I do understand." Elizabeth offered her most winning smile. "My name is Lady Elizabeth Hawthorne, and I wouldn't normally ask if it weren't a matter of great urgency."

The librarian set aside her pencil. "Of course. This way, if you please, my lady." She rose and led them to a small alcove where a black candlestick telephone sat. The librarian spoke briefly to the exchange, then passed the receiver to Elizabeth. "The operator is ready for your number, my lady."

"The Delacourt residence on Lewes Crescent, please."

"I'm afraid that line is engaged, madam." The telephone operator's voice crackled down the line.

"Would you try again?" The librarian watched from her desk, her lips pursed in disapproval.

Another attempt brought the same response. Elizabeth shook her head as she caught Meli's eye.

After a third try, Elizabeth thanked the operator and replaced the receiver in its cradle before returning to the librarian's desk. "Thank you for allowing me to use the telephone."

Elizabeth turned to Meli. "We'll have to go to Rosalind's house." They hurried from the library back to Gigi's Vauxhall.

Elizabeth had the engine running before Meli's door closed, then swiftly merged the motorcar into the Brighton traffic.

"Delilah?" Meli frowned. "Why that name?"

"Who knows? Perhaps he felt Rosalind embodied the same qualities as the Biblical seductress."

"But why give Rosalind a pseudonym when he used their names for the others?"

"Using a pseudonym might have helped him distance himself, making it less personal, more clinical."

Elizabeth steered through the narrow streets past the Royal Pavilion.

"I still don't understand why he singled out Rosalind. She's not a criminal like the others."

"The society columns have been speculating about the nature of Rosalind and Stacey's relationship." Elizabeth cast a quick glance at Meli. "If they were to marry, then I'm sure Sir Lionel would consider someone like Rosalind as a threat to the Grimwald name."

"That's absurd. Everyone knows it's Tommy she has her eye on. She and Stacey are just friends."

"I agree, but clearly Sir Lionel isn't thinking rationally about any of this."

Elizabeth eased off the accelerator as they entered the sweeping curve of Lewes Crescent, bringing the car to a halt outside Rosalind's house.

Elizabeth took the front steps two at a time, Meli close behind her. She pressed the bell, the chime echoing through the house as she shifted her weight from foot to foot.

"Come on, come on." Her fingers drummed against the smooth leather of her handbag.

A maid opened the door, her cap askew. Through the entrance hall, staff rushed back and forth, urgent whispers carrying from the open sitting-room door where the butler's silhouette bent over the sofa.

"Miss Delacourt?"

"In the sitting-room, my lady. Something dreadful's happened–"

Elizabeth brushed past her, Meli at her side. Rosalind lay against the silk cushions, her face deathly pale, while a maid huddled in the armchair, fingers white around a crystal tumbler of brandy.

"What's happened?" Elizabeth crossed to the sofa.

"Someone left flowers on the doorstep." Rosalind gestured to the overturned box on the side table. "Agnes always checks them first because of my allergy. When she opened the corsage box…" Her voice trailed off as she glanced at the maid in the armchair.

Agnes lifted the crystal tumbler with shaking hands. "Three bees flew out, miss; there might have been more." She pushed up her sleeve to reveal an angry welt on her forearm.

"The box?" Elizabeth asked. "Was there a card?"

Agnes shook her head. "No, miss. No florist's mark either."

"I could have died." Rosalind held out her empty tumbler for a refill. "If Agnes hadn't checked that box first … I told you someone's out to get me."

Meli drew Elizabeth aside, her voice low. "Last night as we were leaving Stacey's house,

Rosalind mentioned her bee allergy; Sir Lionel could easily have overheard."

"I know." Elizabeth studied the corsage box. "But finding bees in a flower arrangement isn't unheard of."

"In a bouquet, perhaps. But three? In a box that size?"

Elizabeth pressed Meli's arm. "Stay with her. Don't mention Sir Lionel or the notebook. I'm going to retrieve it."

"You can't go there alone; it's not safe."

"What choice do we have? He has to be stopped, and without that notebook, we have nothing to back up our theory."

"But how are you going to get it?"

"I'll think of something." Elizabeth turned to leave.

"Elizabeth ... you will be careful, won't you?"

"Of course." Elizabeth held Meli's gaze.

She slipped from the house, her mind churning as she made her way along Lewes Crescent to Sussex Square – barely two minutes on foot from Rosalind's house. She had no plan beyond getting into Sir Lionel's bedroom and retrieving the notebook ... no excuse for her presence and no strategy if he was home.

She paused at the wrought-iron gate of Sir Lionel's house, her fingers resting on the latch.

Drawing in a deep breath, she lifted the latch and climbed the steps to the front door.

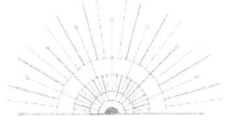

Chapter Twenty-Two

ELIZABETH'S FINGER HOVERED OVER Sir Lionel's brass doorbell. The garden gate clicked shut behind her with metallic finality ... no retreat now. Each breath drew in the cloying sweetness of June roses flanking the stone steps, their perfume a bitter reminder of the corsage box that had nearly sealed Rosalind's fate. A bee flitted between the blooms – one small creature with the power to kill, if employed with sufficient calculation.

Wilson opened the door, his expression warming with recognition. "My lady."

"Good afternoon, Wilson." Elizabeth tilted her head, her smile carrying a hint of apologetic charm. "I hope I'm not calling at an inconvenient time?"

"Not at all, my lady. Though I'm afraid Mr Eustace isn't at home this afternoon."

"Actually, Wilson…" Elizabeth's fingers brushed her earlobe. "After dinner last night, I discovered I'd lost an earring. I wondered if perhaps one of the maids might have found it while tidying?"

"Of course, my lady. Please, come in while I speak with Mrs Roberts." Wilson stepped aside, gesturing Elizabeth into the entrance hall, before disappearing down the passage towards the kitchen.

The maid from the previous evening appeared, her fingers worrying the edge of her apron. "Begging your pardon, my lady. Mr Wilson's attending to an emergency with the kitchen pipes. I've spoken to Mrs Roberts, and no one's mentioned finding an earring, but if it turns up, we'll be sure to let Mr Eustace know straight away."

"I wouldn't normally make such a fuss, but they belonged to my late mother. Would it be possible for me to have a quick look myself?"

"I could search for you, my lady–" The maid startled at a crash from below stairs.

"I can see you're busy, and I hate to be a nuisance, but I was hoping to wear them tonight. I am having a family dinner." Elizabeth took a step towards the main staircase. "Would it be terribly forward of me to have a look myself? I remember having both earrings when I went upstairs to rest."

"I couldn't… it wouldn't be proper, my lady." The maid hurried to catch up as Elizabeth started up the stairs.

"Is Sir Lionel at home today?" Elizabeth kept her pace steady.

"No, my lady. His lordship is in chambers until this evening."

"More buckets." The distant shout drew the maid's attention back towards the kitchen.

"It sounds like you're needed downstairs. I'll be perfectly fine searching on my own."

The maid glanced between Elizabeth and the kitchen as another crash echoed from below.

"If you're sure, my lady?"

"Absolutely."

The maid's footsteps faded down the stairs as Elizabeth crept along the landing towards Sir Lionel's bedroom. Two hairpins from her handbag made quick work of the lock, and after a final glance along the landing, she eased the door open and slipped inside.

Elizabeth crossed to the bureau, tugging at the private compartment where Sir Lionel kept his notebook. The first hairpin slid into position, but the second kept catching on something deep inside the mechanism. Her fingers twitched with every tick of the mantel clock, each strike reminding her of another second lost.

She adjusted the hairpin's angle, pressing deeper until the mechanism released. Elizabeth's shoulders dropped when the compartment opened, but the notebook was gone. She reached inside for the ring, holding the gaudy piece between her fingers. With the notebook gone, she had no real evidence to present to the Chief Inspector, but at least this ring placed Sir Lionel in Vale's studio on the night of the murder.

But if she could just find that notebook, she would have the evidence she needed. She pulled out the first drawer, then the second.

"Looking for this, Lady Elizabeth?"

Her breath hitched at the sound of the key turning in the lock.

She slipped the ring into her pocket and turned. Sir Lionel stood in front of the door, the notebook between his fingers.

"Did you imagine I wouldn't notice the ink spill on my desk?" Sir Lionel's gaze held hers. "One doesn't reach the High Court bench, Lady Elizabeth, by overlooking evidence placed directly before one's eyes."

"Is that what happened with Nathaniel Greaves? Did the police miss vital evidence? Or Matilda Cray?" Elizabeth kept her eyes trained on Sir Lionel as her hand slid closer to her handbag clasp. "Is that why you took matters into your own hands? To ensure they paid for their crimes when the law failed to hold them accountable?"

"Save your pity for those who deserve it." Sir Lionel took another step into the room. "Greaves removed safety protocols to speed up production, causing the death of three workers in that grain press." His fingers tightened on the notebook. "And Cray? You'd grant her sympathy after what she did to those women … and the unborn?"

"And you think that gives you the right to play God?"

"Tell me, Lady Elizabeth, do you believe Brown should have escaped justice after murdering four women for their inheritance? Should he have walked free?"

"Of course not. But it wasn't for you to decide his fate."

"These people are the lowest of the low. They have no place in a civilised society. They must be held accountable."

The irony of his words struck Elizabeth. A judge who had appointed himself executioner, speaking of accountability. "And Vale?" She had no proof he'd killed Vale, but she needed that confession. "What egregious crime had he committed that warranted his death?"

Sir Lionel's eyes blazed at Vale's name. "That worthless excuse for a human being. He was a drunk, a womaniser, a cheater … everything that's wrong with society today."

"Or was it because you found out Vale was Stacey's father?"

Sir Lionel took a step closer as Elizabeth backed away, her hand inching inside her bag. He closed his eyes, drawing in a deep breath.

"Eustace is *my* son." His face twisted, spittle forming at the corners of his mouth. "Alice lied. He *is* my son, do you hear me? Mine."

Elizabeth's breath caught as the truth crystallised. "Alice never left for America, did she? You killed her."

"She left me no choice. She was going to take my son away. A married woman conducting herself like that, flaunting her affair…" His jaw tightened. "She brought it on herself."

"Not another step." Elizabeth drew her Browning Pocket Pistol, both hands steady on the grip. "You speak of evil in others, and yet it is your own hand that sows it."

"You understand nothing." His eyes narrowed. "You don't know what it's like … day after day. These people … they poison our society. Everything I've done, I've done to protect what's right, what's decent."

"A murderer passing judgment on murderers."

"No!" The word burst from him. "I am nothing like them. Nothing. I am the law. I am justice." His fingers raked through his silver hair as he paced the length of the Persian rug.

"After what you've done, it's not the earthly courts you should be worried about."

"I am ready to meet my Maker, Lady Elizabeth." His head snapped towards her, something feral in his gaze as he lunged for her. "The question is, are you?"

The pistol slipped from Elizabeth's grasp, skidding across the floor as Sir Lionel slammed into her. Her skull cracked against the floorboards, lungs emptying in a rush. His weight crushed down, knees pinning her arms as his hands locked around her throat.

Elizabeth thrashed beneath him, but his body weight kept her trapped. Dark spots bloomed across her vision as her chest screamed for air. His grip faltered, the strength leaving his fingers as his own breath grew ragged with exertion.

Just as consciousness began to fade, Sir Lionel rolled off her, his own breath coming in desperate gasps.

The notebook lay just beyond her reach, its pages splayed against the floorboards. Elizabeth pushed herself forward, every breath searing her lungs as she reached for it.

The door splintered inward. Elizabeth's fingers closed around the notebook as Pembroke burst through, Chief Inspector Walsh at his heels.

Pembroke scooped up the pistol, his gaze darting between Elizabeth and Sir Lionel. "Lady Elizabeth, are you all right?"

"A trifle breathless," she managed between gasps. "But otherwise I'm perfectly fine."

Meli slipped past the Chief Inspector and crossed to Elizabeth, her arm sliding around Elizabeth's waist as she guided her to the bed.

The Chief Inspector gestured to the two constables hovering in the doorway. "See to Sir Lionel." They hauled the judge to his feet, his chest still heaving. One reached for his handcuffs. "That won't be necessary." His tone carried steel beneath the courtesy. "Will it, Sir Lionel?"

"I'll have your badge for this–" He doubled over as a cough tore through him. "–for this, Walsh."

"Take him away." He waved away Sir Lionel's words.

"Before you say anything." Meli kept her voice low. "I didn't contact the Chief Inspector."

"If you didn't telephone him, then what's he doing here?"

Meli's fingers twisted a loose thread on the eiderdown. "I'm assuming Pembroke telephoned him."

"But how did Pembroke know?"

"I telephoned him." Meli's words tumbled out. "I was worried about you, and I knew the Chief Inspector wouldn't believe me if I told him about Sir Lionel and the murders, but I had to do something."

"A word, Lady Elizabeth, if you please." The Chief Inspector's customary brusqueness had returned.

Elizabeth clutched the notebook tight as she rose. "Of course, Chief Inspector."

Maids and footmen clustered along the landing, their whispers falling silent as Elizabeth emerged. From the back stairs, more faces peered around the corner.

"Back to your duties, all of you." Mrs Roberts clapped her hands, sending the staff scurrying back to their posts.

Elizabeth crossed to where the Chief Inspector waited by the banister, steeling herself for another lecture about amateur interference in police matters.

"While I don't condone amateurs interfering in police investigations, it seems I'm guilty of the very thing I accused you of – letting sentiment cloud judgment." He slipped his hands into his trouser pockets, rocking on the balls of his feet

Elizabeth placed the notebook in his palm, then retrieved the ring from her pocket. "Alice Grimwald's ring. It appears she never left for America after all. And it places Sir Lionel at Vale's studio on the night of the murder."

"I'll arrange to take a full statement from you when you're feeling better." He studied the ring for a moment before pocketing it. "Would you like me to arrange for a police car to take you home?"

"That won't be necessary, Chief Inspector." Pembroke swept his arm toward the stairs. "I'll see Lady Elizabeth and Miss Diomaros home."

Meli leaned closer, her words meant for Elizabeth's ears only. "Unless I'm very much mistaken, that almost sounded like an apology from the Chief Inspector."

"Let's not get too carried away, shall we?" Elizabeth's lips twitched. "I'm sure an apology from the Chief Inspector is about as rare as a sighting of Halley's Comet."

Pembroke's voice softened as they descended the stairs. "I owe you both a debt I can never repay. The risks you took to clear Essie's name... If you ever need anything, either of you, you only need ask."

"Elizabeth glanced up at him. "Speaking of risks, something's been puzzling me about the break-in at Vale's studio."

"Perhaps someone thought such beauty deserved a more appreciative audience." The twinkle in Pembroke's eye left little doubt as to the portrait's current owner.

Elizabeth watched Pembroke continue down the stairs, thinking of all Essie had endured

… the scandal in Tuscany, losing her child, Vale's cruel manipulation, followed by a murder charge. At last, now she could begin to heal.

While society craved beauty, and men sought to possess it, such gifts could indeed become a curse, as Alice Grimwald had discovered at too high a price.

But Essie had found something rarer – a man who looked past surface beauty and cherished the tender heart beating beneath.

And what of Sir Lionel? How ironic that someone who'd built his life dispensing justice from behind the bench should prove himself so contemptuous of the very law he claimed to defend. His rigid certainty had destroyed so many lives, all while believing himself above the very principles he'd sworn to uphold.

In the end, his carefully constructed facade of respectability had crumbled, revealing a truth as old as time itself … absolute power corrupts absolutely.

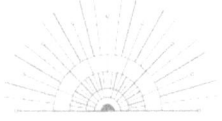

Chapter Twenty-Three

Elizabeth and Meli strolled along Brighton's Palace Pier, keeping to the shaded side where the morning crowds were thinner.

"I can't believe we're leaving tomorrow." Meli glanced at Elizabeth. "It feels like we've only just arrived."

"The prospect of my own bed holds considerable appeal." Elizabeth's fingers drifted to the silk scarf at her neck. "Though I do wish we'd had more time with Gigi. We've hardly seen her with everything that's been going on."

Elizabeth's steps slowed as a man carrying a stack of canvases toward Vivi's gallery crossed in front of them. Had it really only been ten days since they'd bumped into Stacey almost in this exact spot?

As they drew closer, Fenn's angular features emerged from behind the wrapped paintings as he shouldered his way through the gallery entrance.

Seconds later, Vivi appeared in the doorway, glancing up and down the pier, her expression brightening when she spotted them. "Lady Elizabeth, Miss Diomaros, what a pleasant surprise."

"We thought we'd take a final turn along the pier before departing tomorrow."

"You're leaving so soon?" Vivi's eyes flicked to the silk scarf knotted around Elizabeth's neck. "I daresay you'll be glad to see the back of Brighton after everything that's happened. Have you heard from Stacey at all since his father, well, you know?"

"He's barely left the hospital since his father's collapse. According to the doctors, the liver has hardened beyond repair, and it's only a matter of days before … Gigi's with him now and the others take turns, doing what they can to lift his spirits."

"Poor Stacey," Meli said. "As if Sir Lionel's illness wasn't enough to bear, there's all this publicity about what he's done."

"Truth be told, a part of me wants Sir Lionel to suffer for what he's done, especially to Alice." Vivi's gaze flitted to the horizon. "Yet I can't help but feel sorry for Stacey and what Sir Lionel's passing will mean for him."

"I can't even imagine what he's going through." Elizabeth's lips tightened at the corners. "To learn your father murdered your mother … it doesn't bear thinking about."

"Indeed, but at least we can give Alice a proper burial now." Vivi's voice caught. "Though after almost two decades in that lake on the Rottingdean estate…" A fine tremor passed through Vivi's shoulders before she straightened.

"But why Rottingdean?" Meli's brow creased.

"That's where they lived until Alice's–" Vivi faltered, lips shaping the next word but not giving it voice. She drew a shallow breath before continuing. "Until she disappeared. Then Sir Lionel bought the house on Sussex Square, and he and Stacey moved there." She turned toward the sea. "Alice always hated Rottingdean, said it was more like a mausoleum than a home. And to think she's been lying there all these years."

A group of holidaymakers passed, their chatter and laughter jarring against the weight of Vivi's words.

"I see Fenn's going to be showing his work at the gallery." Elizabeth nodded toward the entrance.

"Yes, we've come to an arrangement." Vivi glanced through the window where Fenn was unpacking his canvases. "Sir Geoffrey won't pursue the matter of Vale passing off Fenn's work as his own, but he's keeping the painting and wants first refusal on all of Fenn's new work. I convinced Fenn that it's better to have Sir Geoffrey as an ally rather than an enemy. And as of today, the gallery will represent him."

"It's certainly a step up from drawing caricatures on the seafront," Meli replied.

"Quite." Vivi nodded her agreement. "Anyway, I must dash. These artists may create masterpieces, but ask them to hang a painting straight and they're utterly lost. It was lovely meeting you both, though I wish the circumstances had been different. Do call again when you're next in Brighton."

"We will indeed." Elizabeth inclined her head.

They continued their walk along the pier, the afternoon sun warming their shoulders.

"Elizabeth, do you think Sir Lionel's illness might explain some of his behaviour, like his warped sense of justice?"

"While I don't think it's wholly to blame, I believe his declining mental health played a part. But those tendencies were always there. Look at what he did to Alice. He murdered her when she tried to leave him, then kept up the pretence she was alive for nearly twenty years, letting her child believe his mother had abandoned him."

"Why do you suppose he targeted Rosalind?"

"Perhaps in his twisted mind, he saw Rosalind as Alice and by getting rid of her, he could somehow rewrite the past." Elizabeth shook her head. "Though I doubt even Sir Lionel truly understood his own motives by then."

"It's all terribly sad, isn't it?" Meli drew in a long breath, her shoulders dropping as she released it. "Enough of all this gloom; let's talk about something more cheerful instead." She linked her arm through Elizabeth's. "I wonder how Essie is faring at Pembroke House?"

"Laurie says his mother can be rather formidable, though his father's illness has softened her somewhat. And with four sons, I rather think she'd welcome another female into the family. Besides, the way Essie looks at Laurie ... well, that alone should win his mother over."

Meli gave Elizabeth's arm a gentle nudge. "Can you believe we've been in Brighton all this time and haven't had so much as a paddle?"

"You're absolutely right." Elizabeth's mouth curved into a smile. "It would be almost scandalous to leave without dipping even a toe in the Channel. But I must warn you, the English Channel is a far cry from the warm waters of the Mediterranean, even in June."

Meli arched a brow. "I'm game if you are."

The floor shifted beneath their feet as they picked their way across the pebbles towards the water's edge. Elizabeth hung back a few steps behind, warmth flooding her chest as she watched her cousin splashing about in the shallows. Meli's shriek echoed down the beach as the bracing water caught her ankles, sending her skipping sideways.

Her family might be scattered … Gigi in Tuscany with Uncle Auggy and Aunt Celeste, Chaz in Nairobi with the Red Cross, her mother's Hellenic family across the Aegean … but some families were worth crossing an ocean for.

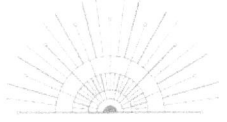

Epilogue

ELIZABETH SETTLED INTO HER favourite armchair, the front page of *The Times* commanding her full attention: BRIGHTON EMBRACES CHANGE AS LIBERAL PEMBROKE UNSEATS CONSERVATIVE STRONGHOLD, dominated the morning's headlines, alongside a photograph that made her smile.

"Winnie, you need to roll over." Meli crouched on the Persian rug, a sliver of sausage poised in her fingers. Winston's tail thumped against the floor as he rolled halfway over, more interested in snacks than theatrics. "No, all the way over. Like this." She rolled over beside him.

Mafdet unfurled her coppery limbs along the window seat cushion, basking in the autumn sunshine. She opened one golden eye to observe Winston's antics, then closed it again with withering judgment.

"Pembroke won his seat." Elizabeth read aloud from the newspaper: "*The Honourable Laurence Pembroke celebrates his historic victory with his fiancée, Miss Esther Baker.*"

She turned the paper so Meli could see Essie standing proudly beside Pembroke outside the Town Hall, her diamond ring clearly visible as her hand rested on his arm.

Elizabeth turned to the society pages. "Ah, Rosalind's portrait is causing quite the stir." Her eyes moved across Mrs Drummond-Ward's *About Town* column.

"*The late Jasper Vale's final work – that scandalously modern portrait of the Honourable Rosalind Delacourt – has sparked fierce competition among private collectors. Whether it's the artist's tragic end or the rather daring pose that commands such interest, this columnist leaves it to her readers' imagination...*"

"I doubt Rosalind will give a fig about the money, though I'm sure she's relishing the scandal it's causing." Meli divided the last of the sausage and placed it in her palm, where Winston snaffled it all in one go. "You know, I never could fathom Vale's obsession with the *Nymphaeum* paintings."

"I believe the series revealed far more about the artist than his subjects. He used classical mythology to disguise something darker – his obsession with corrupting what he worshipped. The purer the subject, the deeper his compulsion to destroy."

"Rather twisted, when you put it like that."

"Quite. Though fitting that his final exhibition revealed his own nature so thoroughly."

Winston rested his head in Meli's lap, eyes half-closed as she scuffed behind his ears. "I wonder how Stacey's getting on in Tuscany."

"The Italian air will be good for him. With all the talk in Brighton about his parents ... well, staying at the villa with Gigi, Uncle Auggy and Aunt Celeste is precisely what he needs. And who knows? He may find his way back to painting."

Voices carried from the entrance hall. Winston's head snapped up, ears forward. The door burst open as Aunt Beatrice swept in, Dalton following in her wake.

"Lady Hawthorne," he announced, slightly breathless.

Elizabeth and Meli exchanged glances. Aunt Beatrice never arrived without sending word ahead.

She sank into the armchair, a few silvery wisps escaping her usually perfect chignon.

"Dalton, some tea, if you please."

"Of course, my lady." The butler withdrew, the drawing room door closing behind him.

Elizabeth crossed to her aunt's chair and knelt beside her, taking her hand. "Aunt Beatrice, whatever's the matter?"

"Oh, Elizabeth … I hardly know where to begin." She drew a ragged breath. "Something quite dreadful has happened…"

If you enjoyed 'Murder at the Palace Pier', then check out Book 7 in the Lady Elizabeth Hawthorne Mystery series,

Murder at Hawthorne Hall

When a stranger arrives at Hawthorne Hall claiming to be the true heir, old secrets threaten to upend everything Aunt Beatrice holds dear. But when the man is found dead, suspicion falls on her—and Elizabeth must uncover the truth before scandal turns to tragedy.

https://books2read.com/u/mg6x7v

Newsletter

Join my Newsletter to receive your FREE copy of Shadow of the Desert Queen, and keep up to date with all the news about new releases, giveaways, promotions, etc.
https://dl.bookfunnel.com/1x00ah4bcx

Dedication

For my crazy, funny, mad, full-on family, who drive me nuts, mostly.
But I wouldn't have it any other way.
xxx

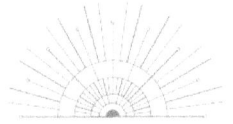

Also by Olivia Rose

MURDER ON THE SS ANDROMEDA

Champagne, caviar, and a side of murder.

When death crashes the party aboard the luxurious SS Andromeda, Lady Elizabeth Hawthorne's mission to escort a priceless Greek artifact to London takes a sinister turn. The captain's mysterious demise plunges Elizabeth into a deadly game of cat and mouse,

where every passenger is a suspect and every smile could mask murderous intent.

Teaming up with lifelong alley, Major Sinclair, Elizabeth dives into a labyrinth of secrets and lies. As they navigate clandestine soirees and whispered conspiracies, the line between ally and adversary blurs. With each uncovered clue, the danger mounts, and trust becomes as fragile as crystal stemware.

Racing against time and a killer's cunning, Elizabeth and Major Sinclair must unravel the twisted web of deceit before the Andromeda docks in Liverpool. But in this floating world of glittering facades and hidden agendas, one misstep could turn their investigation deadly.

Can Elizabeth unmask the murderer lurking among the elite, or will she become the next victim in this high-stakes game of death on the high seas?

https://books2read.com/u/bpnBjX

MURDER AT MAYFIELD MANOR

Blackmail, betrayal and a body in the bath.

Lady Elizabeth Hawthorne's joyous reunion with childhood friend Clemmi Mayfield takes a sinister turn when she uncovers a chilling web of secrets: a hidden marriage, vicious blackmail, and the Countess Magdalena von Habsfeld dead in her bath.

As a relentless blizzard seals the manor, trapping guests and their dark pasts within its frozen walls, suspicion falls on everyone – including Clemmi herself.

Once again thrust into an uneasy alliance with the enigmatic Jonathan Ashcroft, Elizabeth plunges into a labyrinth of decades-old secrets and fresh betrayals. With each revelation, the danger mounts, and she realizes that in this house of lies, even her closest friend could be a deadly enemy.

Racing against both the clock and the elements, Elizabeth must unravel the twisted threads of deceit before the killer strikes again.

But in this snow-bound manor of secrets and shadows, can Elizabeth unmask the killer before she becomes the final victim?

https://books2read.com/u/mlMzDA

MURDER ON THE FRENCH RIVIERA

Diamonds, deceit, and a deadly masquerade.

A scandalous royal murder shatters the Hawthorne family's Riviera holiday, crushing Aunt Beatrice's hopes for her cash-strapped nephew, Alexander, the Earl of Wexford, to marry the Italian princess and save his crumbling estate.

Faced with international scrutiny, the Chief Inspector hastily pins the gruesome crime on the Earl, branding him a murderous fortune hunter.

Refusing to let Alexander fall victim to the Chief Inspector's machinations, Elizabeth and her audacious cousin Meli plunge headlong into a high-stakes investigation. As they peel back the glittering veneer of Riviera society, they uncover a sinister tapestry of betrayal, blackmail, and deadly alliances. With each revelation, the danger mounts, and the cousins find themselves caught in a treacherous game where one false move could cost them everything.

With Alexander's freedom at stake and a looming scandal threatening to ruin the family's reputation, Elizabeth must unmask the true murderer before the Earl's fate is sealed forever.

But in this gilded cage of luxury and vice, can she trust anyone?

https://books2read.com/u/4A1JPp

MURDER AT THE GRAND NATIONAL

Horses, high stakes, and a homicide at the hurdles.

When the 1924 Grand National ends in tragedy, Lady Elizabeth Hawthorne finds herself embroiled in a deadly conspiracy that reaches far beyond the racetrack.

As the dust settles on Aintree's hallowed turf, celebrated jockey Reggie Black lies dead, and Alfie – a former stable boy from Hawthorne Hall – stands accused of murder. Convinced of Alfie's innocence, Elizabeth is determined to uncover the truth.

With a Chief Inspector eager to close the case and the enigmatic Jonathan Ashcroft, whose true motives grow increasingly suspect with each encounter, Elizabeth must navigate a treacherous course. Every step brings her closer to a truth that powerful forces want buried – and puts her squarely in the crosshairs of a killer who'll stop at nothing to keep their secrets.

In a world where fortunes are won and lost on the turn of a hoof, Elizabeth is about to discover that the deadliest wagers are made far from the finish line. Can she unmask the true culprit before the killer strikes again, or will her pursuit of justice lead her to a fate worse than Becher's Brook?

https://books2read.com/u/bzwZZZ

MURDER AT THE OBSERVATORY

Galaxies, guile, and a deadly night sky.

When a rare celestial event ends in tragedy, Lady Elizabeth Hawthorne's island retreat becomes a deadly paradise. The celebrated astronomer Professor Magnus Whitaker is found dead – an apparent suicide after a humiliating failure. But the constellation of clues points to a more sinister truth.

With each guest harbouring their own dark matter, she must navigate a treacherous maze of lies and betrayal. As whispers of blackmail and long-buried secrets orbit the secluded island, the line between ally and adversary blurs like a distant nebula.

With the cosmic clock ticking and danger lurking in every shadow, Elizabeth must align the stars of truth before the killer strikes again. In this deadly game of celestial chess, can she outmanoeuvre a killer who seems to map the sphere with deadly precision? Or will she be eclipsed by their murderous machinations?

https://books2read.com/u/mg6x7v

MURDER AT THE PALACE PIER

Artists, aristocrats, and a masterclass in murder.

Swept into Brighton's dazzling world of artists' studios and bohemian nights by her free-spirited cousin Gigi, Lady Elizabeth's summer takes a dark turn when a renowned artist is found dead on the Palace Pier. Worse still, Gigi's closest friend – a celebrated model on the brink of a prestigious engagement – stands accused of his murder.

As Elizabeth delves deeper, she uncovers a masterpiece of deception spanning a decade – an illicit affair, a desperate cover-up, and a web of forgery that entangles both the criminal underworld and aristocratic society.

With suspects ranging from a vengeful rival artist to a blackmailed lord, Elizabeth must separate genuine clues from clever forgeries. Each revelation paints a darker picture, and someone is determined to keep the truth hidden behind a carefully crafted canvas of lies.

In Brighton's glittering art scene, Elizabeth must expose a killer driven to murder by an artist's brush. But with every suspect concealing their own dark canvas, will she uncover the killer's signature – or become their final masterpiece?

https://books2read.com/u/b50Pn6

MURDER AT HAWTHORNE HALL

Birthright, bigamy, and betrayal.

When a mysterious claimant arrives at Hawthorne Hall declaring himself the rightful heir, Aunt Beatrice's world crumbles. His evidence of her late husband's previous marriage threatens everything she holds dear – her family, her home, and four decades of devoted widowhood.

But when the claimant is found murdered, Aunt Beatrice becomes the prime suspect.

Trapped between family loyalty and mounting evidence, Elizabeth races to uncover the truth about her Uncle Arthur's past, and soon discovers even the most steadfast love can hide the darkest secrets.

With the Hawthorne legacy at stake and her beloved aunt facing the gallows, can Elizabeth expose Arthur's secrets before his past destroys them all?

https://books2read.com/u/bwDWV9

MELI'S MISADVENTURES

THE MISFORTUNE OF THE MAHA-RANI'S TEAR

Diamonds, desire and a Maharani's curse.

When the Maharani's Tear – a priceless diamond steeped in legend and tragedy – vanishes from Wembley's Indian Pavilion, suspicion falls on a young Greek immigrant. But Meli knows better.

Reunited with Dimitri, a friend from her own misadventure aboard the SS Andromeda, she's convinced his friend is innocent. With her faithful companion Winston at her side, Meli delves into a world of Indian princes, arranged marriages, and ancient curses.

As she navigates the dazzling displays and shadowy corners of the Exhibition, she begins to suspect the truth behind the theft is far more complex than Scotland Yard believes.

With royal tempers flaring and the threat of false justice looming, can Meli uncover the truth before an innocent man becomes the latest victim of the Maharani's curse?

https://books2read.com/u/mgnBA7

About the Author

Born and raised in Wales, Olivia and her husband relocated to the Mediterranean island of Cyprus twenty years ago with their two children.

Sharing their home with five cats, two dogs, and a small colony of indigenous creepy crawlies means life is never dull.

Olivia's new series, Lady Elizabeth Hawthorne Mysteries, transports readers back in time to the vibrant and sophisticated world of 1920s England through the captivating tales of Lady Elizabeth Hawthorne. The daughter of an English lord and a Grecian adventuress, Elizabeth's lineage is as rich as the mysteries she uncovers. Her innate passion for archaeology, a legacy from her parents, propels her into a realm filled with ancient secrets and high-society intrigue.

Printed in Dunstable, United Kingdom